The Sentient

Book I of The Sentient Prophecy

Jessica Crawford

This is a work of fictions. Names, characters, places, and incidents either are the product of the author's imagination or are used fictitiously. Any resemblance to actual persons, living or dead, events, or locales is entirely coincidental.

ISBN-10: 0615992625
ISBN-13: 978-0615992624
Trenton Lane

DEDICATION

This one's for Sue and Maude

CONTENTS

Acknowledgments

ACKNOWLEDGMENTS

Many thanks to beta readers extraordinaire Megan Kenny and Danielle Caryl, to Kristy Ellsworth for editing help, to Corey Wright for designing the book cover, and to author M. R. Pritchard for all of her teaching, assistance, and the inspiration to see this through.

1

July 23rd, 2013

They say you don't know what you have until it's gone.

I'm still not entirely sure what it was exactly that I had, if I'm being perfectly honest. Maybe it never was really mine to begin with and I have been deceiving myself all this time. Does that really make any difference, though? As long as you believe something to be true you react the same, feel the same, if it is or it isn't. And isn't that what counts in the end?

The point is *something* is gone, and though I may not fully understand its exact nature and all of the implications, the harsh and undeniable truth is that I have been left feeling empty. Alone.

Lost.

It's ridiculous, really. I should be thanking my lucky stars. I should sprint out these doors and kiss the earth, cartwheel myself away from this place, throw the middle finger over my shoulder for good measure. *Goodbye and good riddance!* Instead I sit rooted here, whiling away the stretching hours writing in this journal, literally aching from the loss of the people I had at one time been hoping to escape.

Hey, I never claimed to be perfect. I haven't exactly been acting rationally since this whole thing started a couple of months ago. The bottom of my world was pulled right out from under me, and as I plummeted through empty space my senses sort of abandoned ship. A sort of mind-numbing self-defense mechanism, I suppose.

If anything, I only feel crazier than ever right now, which is one reason I decided to start writing things down. It's my hope that putting into words all of the thoughts that have been thrashing around in my brain, the emotions straining beneath the surface of my skin, might help me to make some sense of them. Maybe this journal will help me to understand the things that have happened, understand how I should be feeling about them. And maybe it will help me see where it is I'm supposed to go from here.

Where do I belong?

It's worth a shot, at least. Otherwise all I do these days is wander these empty halls, searching for clues and hidden messages that may not even be there. As you can imagine, that doesn't do much for an already-wounded psyche.

And so here goes nothing.

It began, as many things do, when something else had come to its end.

I fidgeted with the thin material of the hospital gown, tucking it more securely around my legs as the doctor pushed past the hanging curtain into the room. His eyes skimmed the clipboard in his hand before alighting on my face. "Miss Cassidy?" I gave a terse nod. "I'm afraid it seems you're miscarrying."

"I…what?" The full meaning of his words didn't reach me at first. I watched them leave his mouth, sensed rather than saw the ugly vibrating airwaves suspended in slow motion between us before smacking me full on in the face. Even then I thought I must have misheard. "I'm sorry, what did you say?"

His eyes had me ensnared, there was no escaping the pitying look they held. "You're losing the baby."

When comprehension finally took root and blossomed, I was stunned. Somewhere amidst the shock there was a trace of embarrassment as well. I'm not proud of that, but it's true.

"I was pregnant? Are you sure?"

More than a year earlier I had stopped taking the pill after developing a blood clot in my leg. I never ended up choosing another form of birth control. I guess at the time maybe I thought an 'accidental' pregnancy might be the solution to the problem with me and Derek. Like we would instantly become one happy little family, all tied up with ribbon. Anyway, I had gone all that time without getting pregnant, and so eventually assumed that, for one reason or another, it just couldn't happen.

The hospitalist glanced down at the papers again. "Positive. There was definitely hCG in your blood, but at very low levels. We can do an ultrasound to make sure there's nothing else going on. You'll probably continue to pass everything on your own over the next few days, but you should take it easy. I can prescribe you some Percocet in the meantime, for the cramping." He met my eyes again. "I'm sorry."

The funny thing was, I was sorry too. I hadn't even known there was a baby. Still, as the doctor handed me the prescription and walked out of the room, I found that I was crying.

The bleeding had started when I was at my job as a registered nurse at the New Beginnings Birth Center in Syracuse, New York. At twenty-five years old I was leading what appeared to be a model life. I had a career that I enjoyed and a boyfriend of five years whom everyone else assumed would be proposing before long.

In reality, Derek and I had come to a point in our relationship where we merely occupied the same space, brushing past each other in the apartment as we went about the business of living. I would go through the movements of my yoga, trying to focus my energy within, while he blared the television in the other room, shouting as if the people on the screen would hear him and respond. Neither of us was the person we once thought the other to be. Whenever we did have to interact I felt like a ghost of his past, insubstantial as his gaze passed through me and my words hung in the air unheard. Our rooms became stifled with the weight of those words. Even worse were the things that went unsaid. Those prowled about the place, just out of sight, but we both knew they were there.

For days I had been prepared for any bleeding, but when the stabbing pains began at work and I hurried to the restroom, I saw that I was passing clots. Alarmed, I hobbled to the nurse's station clutching at my abdomen, and told my coworkers what was going on. Chantell, one of the midwives, lowered her chin and looked at me over the rim of her eyeglasses.

"You need to get on over to the ER and get checked out, hon," she chastised. "I'm sure the others'll cover your patients for you." I'm certain they all knew the truth before I did.

The birthing center and the hospital were directly across the street from one another, connected by an underground tunnel. They were affiliated, but the former appeared as a standalone building, making it more attractive to expectant mothers who wanted to experience labor and delivery in a more comfortable, home-like setting. The tunnel allowed for quick access in the event something went wrong at a delivery and the services of the NICU were needed.

This was the route I took to get to the emergency department. On the way there my mind scanned through all of the terrible diseases and disorders I was surely suffering from. The obvious answer didn't even occur to me.

After submitting to some blood work and an ultrasound, the hospitalist broke the news to me. And with it, he broke my heart.

Derek barely reacted when I told him the news. For a brief time I even considered not telling him at all. When I did, it was like presenting him with a problem and a solution all at once, one cancelling the other out. For a fleeting moment he looked dumbstruck. "Huh," was all he managed to say before zoning back in on his smart phone.

Our relationship didn't last very long after that. It was as if I had tumbled down into a hole that I couldn't scrabble my way out of, and while trapped there I could only feel in turns depressed and angry. Angry at Derek. Angry at myself. I wanted out of that hole, I wanted to feel normal again. Trouble was, I wasn't sure I remembered what normal felt like anymore. I realized that I couldn't think of the last time I had felt at peace with life and my lot in it.

For his part, Derek was constantly losing his temper with me for moping around about losing a baby we hadn't even wanted in the first place. He threw his hands in the air and declared that he couldn't understand me anymore.

Another surprise pregnancy wasn't a concern at the time, since through mutual aversion there wasn't even the slightest physical contact between us. Moments of intimacy were few and far between even before the miscarriage; now, they were nonexistent. Finally, Derek mentioned that the lease to our apartment was due to expire in another month, and he informed me of his plan to move in with one of his old high school buddies. Neither one of us brought up the idea of me going with him. As far as breakups go, the end itself was actually relatively painless. Derek moved out the next week and that, as they say, was that.

When I first returned to work after the miscarriage, my coworkers were all very kind and offered their condolences. At one point I mentioned that I hadn't even noticed any symptoms, not a single heave of morning sickness. Chantell explained to me that sometimes the absence of symptoms is actually a sign of a pregnancy doomed from the start. Women who get violently sick are much less likely to lose the baby. She also reassured me that these things are often flukes, and chances were low that it would happen again.

I began picking up extra shifts at work. The alternative was to shuffle around the half-emptied apartment with only our cat, Dinah, for company. I would have challenged Derek to a fight to the death before letting him take the cat with him, but he never even brought it up. She, apparently, was expendable to him. Absurd as it may sound, I was more hurt for her than I was for myself.

I could tell people at work thought I was poised to go off the deep end. A few times I glanced up and caught them quickly averting their eyes. I have to admit I was rather distracted those days. I remember a time I was documenting in a patient's chart when my mind must have drifted and I zoned out. The sound of a baby beginning to yowl in one of the patient rooms jarred me from my reverie, and when I looked back down to what I had been writing I saw it was complete gibberish. Since it was part of a legal record and others had previously documented on the same sheet, I couldn't discard it and start fresh. I had to strike a single line through everything I had written, then next to all of the nonsense jot the word "error", followed by my initials. My madness forever memorialized.

Another couple of weeks passed. I moved through the motions of life, all the while drowning inside of myself.

And then everything changed.

When I arrived at work one morning, the night nurse reporting off told me about the patients I would be caring for that day. There was a woman who had arrived a few hours before in the early stages of labor. This was her third child, and so there was the possibility that she would progress rapidly.

And then there was the woman in Room 5, who had delivered the previous evening. Every baby in the birth center rooms-in with his or her mother rather than being taken to a nursery. All this woman and her child would need from me was to check in on them periodically throughout the day to make sure everyone was healthy and adjusting to their new roles.

I looked in on the laboring woman first. Her demeanor was chipper as she introduced herself and her husband, told me about the baby girl they were expecting and described what her nursery at home was decorated like. Three times she interrupted her stream of chatter to hold rigid hands to her abdomen and focus on taking deep breaths, blowing them out through trembling lips. This woman was putting up a good front, but I had my suspicions that she might be having a baby before lunchtime. When I asked what I could do for her, all she requested was a fresh pitcher of water. I brought one to her, instructed her to send her husband out to fetch me should she need anything else, and moved on to see my next patient.

I tapped on the door of Room 5, not wanting to make too much noise in case the new mother and her baby were asleep.

They weren't sleeping. Instead, when I stepped into the room I was greeted by the sight of a slight woman perched stiffly on the edge of the room's queen-sized bed, clutching her baby to her body. I knew from reading her chart that her name was Cassandra Dorn, and she was my age. Where there was space for the name of the father of the baby, the words "Not Involved" were scrawled. What the chart couldn't have told me was that she was uncannily beautiful. Auburn hair poured down her back and around slim shoulders, managing to gleam even in the dim lowlights of the birthing suite. Eyebrows arched over glistening eyes, and her skin was porcelain imbued with life.

She was stunning, and she was terrified.

Her face was the same pallid shade of the rumpled bed sheets, even her lips had been sapped of all color. Her delicate chin quivered, her eyes were painted with a sheen of tears. The blatant look of fright on her face forced me back a step. Before I could go any further she sprung from the bed and crossed the dark hardwood floor, closing the distance between us. She thrust the baby against my chest.

"Please," she whispered, her eyes searching mine. "Please, take him!"

My arms had automatically reached around the swaddled bundle. I glanced down at the face of the child and back up to his mother.

"Take...what do you...I mean-" I was choking on my words. I looked back down to the baby while I tried to gather myself. Clearly this was not a simple case of a weary new mother who wanted her child taken out of the room so that she could get some sleep. I pulled myself together and tried to form a coherent response. "Ms. Dorn, are you afraid you might harm your baby?" Such things were not unheard of in severe cases of postpartum depression or psychosis.

She clamped her lips together as she lowered her gaze to her infant son. The tears spilled over and began to course freely down her face. "Not *me*," she answered.

An unfamiliar sensation flourished inside of me, like ice forming on the surfaces of my gut. I thought about what she was telling me. "Is someone else going to hurt the baby?" I was whispering now, too.

She lifted her eyes back to mine and parted her lips, but before she could speak, something drew her attention to the doorway behind me. Her pupils constricted and her mouth snapped shut.

Twisting around, I saw a man standing in the threshold. Appearing to be in his mid-thirties, the visitor had a neatly trimmed beard and sported a button-down shirt tucked into dark slacks. The russet shade of his hair matched Cassandra's so exactly that I immediately understood him to be a relative of hers.

"Ah! I see my dear sister is showing off her little princeling already. Handsome little brat, isn't he?" The man strode over and placed himself between Cassandra and myself. The scent that pervaded the room when he entered made me think of that almost spicy way the woods smell in wintertime. Earthy, and cold. He tugged the knit cap from the baby's head, revealing downy hair black as tar. "Other than the hair color, it seems he has inherited his mother's genes. Which, believe me, is much more fortunate than the alternative." I looked to Cassandra, whose eyes were trained on the floor.

"But I forget my manners!" the man declared. "Allow me to introduce myself. I have the pleasure of being Victor Dorn, Cassandra's eldest brother." He extended a hand to me. Unsure of what to do, I hesitated before handing the child back to his mother in order to meet Victor's handshake. His grip was soft and cool. I suppressed the urge to shudder.

"Anna Cassidy," I returned, meeting his penetrating gaze. He was smiling, baring teeth that were very straight and very white. So perfect as to seem almost unnatural.

"Charmed," he replied. My hand dropped to my side as he released it and turned toward his sister. "Well, Ms. Cassidy, thank you for taking care of Cassandra, but I'm sure you must have other patients to attend to now. If you don't mind, my sweet sister and I have...family matters to discuss."

Cassandra was staring at the baby in her arms. Her tears had stopped, her jaw had tensed. There was now an edge of restrained anger in her face.

"Ms. Dorn, is there anything else I can do for you?" I asked, making a point of not looking at the brother or acknowledging the fact that he had just, in effect, dismissed me.

"No," she muttered. "Nothing else."

I felt confused. I felt impotent. Not knowing what else I could do, I turned on my heel and left the room. The door clicked shut behind me.

What the hell just happened in there?

I paused in the hall for a moment to collect myself before making my way to the nurse's station. I decided to take another look at Cassandra Dorn's chart to see if it held any information that could provide me with clues to what that little scene had been about. I was left disappointed. The only thing new to be learned was that there was an unusual lack of information on this woman. Her paperwork showed that she had received no prenatal care. She had simply shown up at the birthing center in full blown labor. There was no chosen pediatrician listed, either.

I slapped my forehead into my palms and let out a sigh of exasperation. Nancy, the charge nurse on duty, swiveled in her chair to face me. "Something wrong, Anna?"

"The patient in Room 5, Dorn. She's worried about her baby. She seems very anxious."

Nancy nodded. "Baby blues, huh? Your first couple of weeks with your new baby are supposed to be full of wonder and joy, and instead so many of us spend them on a hormonal roller coaster ride."

"I don't know, Nance. I think this might be something more."

Nancy had turned back to the pile of papers needing her attention. "Well, if you're really concerned we could always have the social worker speak with her when she makes her rounds later today."

I glanced back toward the closed door to Room 5. "Yeah, maybe that would be a good idea."

Before I had a chance to do any more thinking on the subject, my other patient's husband stuck his head out into the hall. "Miss? My wife is asking for you." No sooner were the words were out of his mouth than his wife's voice could be heard screeching, "Stephen, what's taking so long? *Stephen!*"

"That's my cue," I mumbled as I pushed myself up out of my chair and made for the room.

"I'll page Chantell for you," Nancy called after me.

Within the next hour the woman had given birth to a healthy daughter. The baby was placed on her mother's chest to get to know her parents while I went about the business of cleaning up after the ordeal. Glancing to check on them, I saw that the mother had her hands wrapped around her new baby, but it was her husband she was looking at. The two were gazing into each other's eyes, absolute bliss reflected from one to the other and back again. Mother, father, and newborn child, all with their own individual roles, but part of something bigger. All exactly where they belonged.

The insane urge to start sobbing rushed over me. Instead, I bit down hard on the inside of my cheek to stem the tears, and set about helping the mother getting her baby to nurse.

By the time I stepped out of the room the social worker had arrived and was talking with Nancy at the desk. I pushed the new family to the back of my mind and brought my attention back around to my other, more worrisome, patient. I edged up to the desk and waited for a lull in the conversation.

"Rosa, when you get a chance, I think the lady in Room 5 might need a consult with you."

"Actually," Nancy interjected, "that patient is gone. She came out asking for early release. You had your hands full with that delivery, but they were adamant about leaving as soon as possible. Nicole was available, so I had her do the discharge for you."

I found myself struck dumb for a moment. "Oh. Okay." Something in her words had bothered me more than the rest. "You said 'they' were adamant?"

"Yes, there was a gentleman with her when she came to the desk."

My mouth must have hung open in dismay. When I could muster no response right away, Nancy and Rosa resumed their chatting.

There was a sinking feeling in my chest. I felt as though I was complicit in some sort of crime, although I couldn't say exactly what. How could I have just meekly walked away from the situation, just because the inexorable force that was Victor Dorn had commanded me to do so? What an idiot I had acted. What a failure I was. I realized with a start that this was a reflection of how I had been feeling about myself for several weeks-months, even: I was a failure. I had had a chance for a loving, happy family of my own, and I had failed. Moisture materialized at the corners of my eyes as I made this connection.

Not wanting my coworkers to think I was even more unhinged than they already did, I swiped at the tears and marched over to where we kept the charts of discharged patients waiting to be dismantled. Cassandra Dorn's was on top. I scooped it up, dropped into a seat, and buried my face in its pages.

There was at least one piece of information yet to be gleaned from the file. We needed the mothers' information upon admission for billing purposes. There on the first sheet was Cassandra's home address. I saw that she lived in Skaneateles, a notably prestigious town located about twenty-five miles outside of the city. The area encompassed several hamlets as well as the picturesque village situated right on the edge of the most pristine of the Finger Lakes. I could easily picture Cassandra and Victor Dorn as part of such an esteemed region.

I grabbed a Post-it note from the desk and scribbled down the address.

"Anna, honey, are you okay?" I heard Nancy ask. Until then I hadn't noticed that my tears had returned unbidden. I leapt up from my seat and tossed the chart back where it belonged, stuffing the Post-it note into my pocket. I didn't want to have to answer any questions about why I was writing down information protected by patient confidentiality regulations.

"I could use a breather," I explained, despising the pinched way my voice came out sounding. "Mind if I head to lunch now?"

"Of course," Nancy answered, her voice uncertain.

I nodded and made my escape.

I can't say I was very surprised when I was told the manager wanted to see me when I returned from lunch. The smile Laurie gave me when I entered her office was a sad one.

"Anna. Thanks for stopping in. How was lunch?"

"It was fine."

She nodded knowingly, not taking her eyes from mine. She took a drawn out breath and leaned back in her chair. "Anna, listen. I know you've been through a lot lately. Of course you're an asset here at the birthing center, but you need to take care of yourself first and foremost." I could feel my face redden. "Why don't you take some time for yourself? Personal time, bereavement time; we'll write it up however we need to."

The thought of not having work to keep myself distracted was not particularly appealing, but I could see where Laurie was coming from. She was probably worried I was going to suffer a complete breakdown while on the job one of these days.

"Okay, Laurie," I conceded, my voice dull even to my own ears. "Whatever you think is best."

Just like that, I no longer had the routine of my job to hold me up anymore, either.

That night at home I fired up my laptop. Dinah wove in and out of my legs purring, glad to no longer be alone in our disaster of an apartment. The lease was up in a matter of days, and I had most everything in boxes. I still wasn't sure about the logistics of the move yet. I have a modest collection of old, rare books. It's a hobby of mine, searching through used book stores for the gems. I had made sure to spread these amongst several different boxes, but still, their weight added up. There was no way I would be able to lift and move all of those boxes on my own.

Then there was the fact that, even though everything was packed up ready to go, I still wasn't sure where it was I would be going.

Once I had logged on to the computer I brought up Google Maps. I tapped in the information from the crumpled Post-it note. The map zoomed to the location right away, but I was taken aback to see that it had added something: before the street address were the words Willow Glen Manor.

A house with a name. We were even swankier than I had realized.

The thought that something awful might happen to a baby had been gnawing at me all day. Through my failure to act, had I resigned that child to some terrible fate? He belonged with his mother, but even she, whose natural place it was to love and care for him, had feared for his safety if he remained with her.

I lay awake in bed for a long time that night, staring at the shadows cavorting on the ceiling. The only time the niggling doubt abated was when I came to a decision, and at once the frantic spinning of my mind quieted, the strain I had been carrying in my body melted into a dull ache. My ability to make judgments at the time was questionable at best, but once I made up my mind I was finally able to settle down to sleep. It was decided.

In the morning I would be paying a visit to Willow Glen Manor.

2

July 24th, 2013

Willow Glen Manor. This place is even more remarkable than I had imagined back when I first learned of its existence.

As I write in this journal I am, in fact, sitting at the oak desk in one of the guest rooms of the manor. And what a room it is. The walls are wood paneled with carved pillars at each corner, the woodwork depicting flowering vines wrapped along the length of each column. Deborah, the housekeeper, once explained to me the wood was walnut. I don't know much about architecture, but that certainly sounded impressive to me.

Deborah also told me the tapestries in the house are Flemish. This guest room, my room, houses my favorite tapestry in the whole place. It shows a woman in a brocade gown, a fringe of red hair peeking out from under her headdress. She stands beside a tall flowering plant. One arm reaches out and she pinches a leaf between slender fingers.

It wasn't until some time after my arrival that I came to understand that some of the furnishings that adorn the walls here are more than they seem. Some convey hidden messages. Several times lately I have found myself drifting through the rooms and the halls of the manor, inspecting the decor up close, hoping to find answers. If any are there, I haven't been able to recognize them. I'm only human, after all.

Even if the red-haired lady in my room is keeping secrets from me, still I find her to be a source of comfort. Sadly, she and the cat are my only company these days. The rest of the house echoes with the absence of the people who once filled it. Where voices hung in the air, now there is only the roar of a forlorn silence.

Did you catch the part about the cat? Yes, Dinah is here with me. At this very moment she is curled up on the large four-poster bed in the room, a black ball of fur sinking into the thick burgundy comforter. At least the cat can sleep comfortably in that bed. For me it brings back uneasy memories that keep me tossing and turning at night, restless. I fear the dreams that come to me in that bed: the ones I wake from filled with dread; and the ones that leave my skin tingling, kindled by the touch of one who is long gone.

You're probably wondering how I ended up here. It's customary for newborns to go to the pediatrician after discharge for weight and jaundice checks. Since Cassandra Dorn's baby did not have a pediatrician, I intended to show up and claim I was there to check up on the baby as part of a public health nursing initiative. I thought it sounded like a pretty reasonable excuse.

Staying had never been part of the plan.

If I hadn't been so mired in dark thoughts, I'm sure I would have been better able to appreciate the beauty of the drive to Willow Glen Manor. Much of the route was through gently sloping wooded hills. It had just occurred to me that I hadn't seen any houses in a while when I came up to a wrought iron gate set into a stone wall. The gate stood open. That fact seemed ominous rather than welcoming, but maybe that had more to do with my guilty conscience for arriving under false pretenses, or my fears of what it was I might find at the end of my journey.

I checked the directions I had printed to verify that I was in the right place. I inched my car through the opening, and as I passed I could see writing carved into the stone of the wall, the same words on either side of the entrance: SCIRE EST MUTARE. I knew enough to recognize it as Latin, but wouldn't understand the meaning until it was explained to me at a later time: to know is to change.

A few minutes after leaving the wall behind, I left the cover of the trees and caught my first sight of the manor house itself. Needless to say, as a fifty room mansion of limestone fronted with soaring columns, the place looked suitably striking, and not just a little imposing. I could feel my pulse hammering as I steered my car along the circular drive and put it into park.

It took some time sitting in my seat staring at the grand building before I had summoned enough courage to step out of the car and make my approach. "Nothing ventured..." I mumbled, counting each step I took in an effort to keep myself distracted as I ascended the stone stairwell. Without allowing time to lose my nerve, I reached out and rang the bell. I wiped sweaty palms on my pant legs while I waited for an answer.

My thoughts of *"maybe no one's at home"* were dashed away as the heavy door swung open with a creak of complaint. The silver-haired bespectacled man who stood revealed on the other side wore a gray vest over a white shirt, dark dress pants, and black shoes that gleamed. He couldn't have looked more like a modern day butler had he tried. "May I help you?" he inquired, his tone polite.

I introduced myself and presented him with the lie I had been practicing during the drive, and hoped I sounded sincere. I finished with, "And so I've come to check up on Cassandra and the baby. Are they at home?"

I must have been pretty convincing, or at least that's what I though at the time, because the butler immediately stood aside and ushered me in. "Right this way, please, Miss."

Beyond the doorway stretched a vast foyer with a floor of marble. Across from the entrance a sprawling staircase swept up to the second floor. I was duly impressed, but had little time to gawk as the butler led me down a dim passage off of the great hall. He stopped in front of a doorway and indicated that I should pass through. "If you would be so kind as to wait in the parlor, Miss. I shall announce your arrival."

The room I had been shepherded into appeared just how I would picture a parlor to look. A striped sofa stood against one wall, flanked by gleaming end tables with curved legs. Two armchairs were arranged along the opposite wall. An ornamental rug spread beneath my feet. The room was all bold colors, greens and reds and blues. A large canvas depicting a stag hunt hung on one wall, a painting of the ruins of a castle overlooking the sea on another. I thought to myself, *When I get myself out of this situation I've blundered into, I can tell people I was actually inside a real-life parlor, like straight out of a romance novel.*

I heard footsteps approaching and spun around. The tread was heavy and purposeful, and I began to suspect the truth before my eyes confirmed it. The person who appeared in the doorway was not Cassandra, but her brother.

Victor flashed his teeth at me as he stepped into the room, but the look in his eyes brought goose bumps to my flesh. "Miss Cassidy," he announced. His hands were clasped behind his back and this time he offered no handshake. "We have been expecting you."

The stories and excuses fled from my mind. "Expecting me?"

Victor took another couple of steps into the room. "Yes. I persuaded my lovely sister to tell us all about the...misguided appeal she made to you, back at the birth center."

Misguided appeal? I didn't understand. Where was Cassandra, and why would she have told Victor about her plea? Unless I had come to an extremely wrong conclusion. I was more confused than ever, but I didn't have time to figure out what was going on and change tactics. The only response I could muster was to stick with my original plan.

"I'm sorry, I'm here to check up on Cassandra and her baby. As a follow-up appointment. She left before I could schedule one with her. If this is a bad time...?"

Victor cocked his head and raised an eyebrow, giving me a look that clearly said, *Now, now, we both know better than that.* I tried to swallow, my throat dry and tight. But I was beginning to get angry as well. Who was this man to intimidate me like this? To make his sister so fearful?

"You needn't worry about Cassandra and the child," he assured me, but there was an unmistakable edge to his voice.

"That's great, but I'd like to assess them for myself. Will they be joining us here?"

"I'm afraid that won't be possible."

I felt my stomach lurch. Had something terrible already happened? That idea alone was upsetting, but for the first time the thought crossed my mind that I may have put myself in real danger as well. Fear overshadowed the anger once more.

"Okay, well. In that case I guess there's no reason for me to be here. I'm sorry to have disturbed you. I'll just be going then."

"That won't be happening either." Victor pulled his hands from behind his back and crossed his arms in front of his chest. I realized with mounting alarm that he stood planted between me and the room's only exit.

I'm sure Victor must have seen the color drain from my face. He stared me down for a moment before dropping his hands to his sides and exhaling heavily. "Do have a seat, Miss Cassidy. What you just said is not entirely true. Despite my own strong feelings on the matter, some of my family is of the opinion that we do, in fact, need you here."

I refused to sit. I didn't want this man to see just how unsettled I really was. I remembered reading that if you were ever attacked by a black bear, playing dead could be a fatal mistake. It was better to put up a fight. The bear might decide you were more trouble than you were worth. Might the same be true with Victor Dorn? Hell if I knew, but it was all I could think to do. I lifted my chin in defiance and said, "I have no idea what you're talking about."

Victor's face twisted into an ugly expression before he explained. "My father has fallen ill. He becomes sicker and weaker with each day that passes. Such an ailment is...unusual for him, and he is alarmed. We all are. No one thus far has been able to do anything for him. And he rarely leaves the house, you see. When he heard that a nurse would be coming here, he requested that you stay to tend to him and attempt to bring him back to health."

"You mean stay to have a look at him and see what suggestions I can make?"

"I mean stay and live here to care for him for however long he requires you to."

I could feel my fingernails scoring marks into the palms of my hands. "I see. And what choice do I have in the matter?" I asked, trying to keep my voice even.

Victor's lips curled up at the corner. "None."

I didn't know what to say. How could any of this be really happening? Somehow, though, I could feel in my bones that Victor Dorn was being gravely serious. I had to tread carefully.

"I'm sorry, but maybe you can explain what, exactly, is going to stop me from just walking out the door and never coming back?"

"You're a nurse. Is it not your duty to care for those in need? Didn't you come all this way out of some sense of responsibility for the welfare of the world and everyone in it?" He was mocking me and I knew it. On the other hand, if staying meant I might have a chance to see Cassandra and her baby, see with my own eyes that they were safe...

Victor continued. "You're practically all ready to move, anyway. Yes. We know your belongings are mostly packed up in boxes. Finding someplace to store them shouldn't present too much of a struggle. Of course you'll need to bring some of the necessities here

21

with you, as it appears you will be staying for an undetermined length of time. And so I think you may leave here today after all. Go home, see to the arrangements. You are to return by tomorrow afternoon." He made as if to leave the room, but as he reached the threshold he paused and craned his neck around to offer one last instruction. "And I don't think I need to tell you not to attempt to flee or to tell anybody about any of this. If you do, we will know."

Back at the apartment, I slammed the door shut behind me and flung my purse to the floor, its contents scattering across the carpet. Damn Victor Dorn and his ability to make me feel so powerless! I made straight for the shower, yanking my clothes off as I went, and spun the knob for hot water. I let the steaming cascade pound against my flesh, hoping it might ease some of the tension coiled up within my every muscle.

As I showered, I considered my options.

I could try to forget about everything that had happened and chalk it up to a family who talked crazy but in the end were harmless. But would a harmless person know the contents of my apartment? That all of my stuff was packed up in boxes? That particular bit of information was thoroughly creeping me out.

I could go to the authorities and tell them I had been threatened. I *had* been threatened, hadn't I? Maybe not in so many words, but there was definitely something not quite right going on with the Dorns. Something menacing, but also somewhat enigmatic. Beguiling. I understood too late that traveling to their home had been like opening Pandora's Box.

Instead, I ended up doing exactly as Victor had told me to do. It chafed, precisely because he had issued it like an order and seemed to have no doubt in his haughty, patronizing mind that I would comply. However, even though he had been taunting me, he had struck a nerve when he talked about duty. I was more certain than ever that Cassandra and her son were in trouble, and maybe this sick father was truly in need of help, too. Could I really turn my back when I might actually be needed somewhere?

Possibly this notion itself would always have been enough to sway me. Even if not, we have already established that I wasn't thinking one hundred percent rationally those days. Already I felt completely uprooted, was floating through my life searching for something solid to grasp onto. And then came the Dorns.

I understood that I might be placing myself in danger by submitting to the demands of someone who had no problem issuing threats to a person he barely knew, a person whose own sister was terrified of him. But people can't see it when you're suffering emotional pain. You find yourself wanting to make what you are enduring manifest somehow, so that others can just look at you and say, "Wow, she's not okay, is she?" Through your actions you show them that something is very wrong. That you are in need of some sort of rescue.

For one of these reasons, or maybe all of them, by the time I stepped from the shower with my skin flushed and dripping water, I knew I would be going back.

I returned to Willow Glen Manor the next day. I brought my clothes, toiletries, what medical equipment and supplies I kept at home, my laptop, my cell phone, and my cat. The essentials. Everything else I stashed at a rental storage facility.

It was the butler who received me again. He introduced himself as Frederick and took my bags. The cat carrier, the occasional low growl emanating through its bars, he left for me to handle. So far Dinah was not pleased with our relocation.

Frederick guided me up the grand staircase and down a corridor. He stopped in front of the door of the guest room that was to be mine for the duration of my stay, however long that might be. "You have a private washroom through the door on the other side of the bed there. The rooms have already been prepared in anticipation of your arrival, but please feel free to make any changes you feel are necessary to make yourself at home," Frederick informed me. I fought the urge to quip, *'Like leaving this place and actually going home?'* Immediately after that thought my spirits sunk when I was forced to acknowledge the fact that I no longer had a home of my own. If I was being honest with myself, I hadn't truly had one for some time.

Frederick lowered my bags to the floor at the foot of the bed and continued. "You may unpack and rest up for a time. The Master requests your presence at dinner at seven o'clock. I will come to fetch you myself." The butler bent at the waist as a means of excusing himself and retraced his steps out of the room and down the hall.

I pushed the door shut behind him and turned to take in my surroundings. Another rumble from the cat carrier in my hands jolted me into action. I set the carrier down and unlatched the door. Dinah crept out, sniffing warily at everything she came across. I had been glad to hear I had my own bathroom. For a while I had been resigned to the fact that I was going to have to keep her litter box right in my bedroom. I went about getting her box set up and placing her food and water dishes.

I pulled out my laptop. Setting it on the great desk hulking beneath the room's window, I hooked up all the cords and got everything plugged in and running. I tried to bring up the internet browser, but a window popped up to inform me that there were no wireless connections in the vicinity. Hopping up from the desk chair, I scanned the walls around me, looking to see if there was cable running into the room anywhere. There was nothing.

It felt like a door had just been slammed shut in my face. I could feel my heart in my throat.

I turned to where I had tossed my purse on top of the bed and dug through it until I pulled my cell phone free. Three bars at the top of the screen indicated that Willow Glen Manor had passable cell phone reception. I was glad to have that link to the outside world, at least. My relief quickly soured, however, when I realized that the battery was nearly dead and I couldn't remember packing the phone charger. Kneeling down, I grabbed the zipper on one of my bags and tugged it open. I rifled through the contents, undoing in a matter of seconds my neat job of folding and organized packing. Not finding the charger, I moved on to ransacking the next bag. Another minute of frenzied searching confirmed what I had already begun to suspect.

I must have packed the phone charger away in one of the boxes at the storage facility. As a result, I had at best two days of battery life left, and that was if I was lucky. Recent events had me believing my luck had long since run out.

"Shit!" I straightened and tossed the phone onto the desk with a clatter. Dinah darted beneath the bed, her tail puffed up to twice its normal size. "Sorry," I muttered. Feeling frustrated with myself, I moved on to putting away the heap of clothes that had formed on the floor, and everything else I had brought with me.

It would be an understatement to say I was nervous about the upcoming dinner, and so of course seven o'clock was upon me before I knew it. I had no idea what sort of dress code applied to a dinner at the Dorn residence, but I had a feeling the sweatpants and tank top that was my norm back at the apartment weren't going to cut it. I decided to risk overdressing rather than under. The dress I chose was a champagne color. It had a fitted bodice with a sweetheart neckline and a knee-length skirt of tulle overlying a satiny lining, a relic from the time when Derek used to take me out to dinner at fancy restaurants. I was making a last ditch attempt to make my hair do something nice when there was a knock at the door. "Coming!" I called over my shoulder.

It was Frederick come to collect me for dinner. Once again he escorted me through the manor house, this time to the dining room.

If I had been pleased to find the parlor looking just as I would have expected, the dining room did not disappoint either. The ceiling soared far overhead, and by craning my neck I could see it was painted with a scene of golden-haired cherubs cavorting on feathery clouds. A massive fireplace graced one end of the room, unlit at that time of year. The dining table reached nearly from one end of the room to the other. I imagined it could easily sit twenty people.

As it was, there were six people seated, all clustered at one end of the table. Clamping my hands together in front of my body to make sure they didn't start shaking, I made my approach.

The man at the end of the table was undoubtedly the head of the family, the father Victor had spoken of. My would-be patient. He had a full head of steely gray hair and a beard to match. It was hard to judge how tall he might be, because at that moment he was hunched forward in his seat, leaning his weight onto his forearms braced against the table. Immediately to his left was Victor, who was missing his infamous grin. In fact, he looked downright peeved. Noticing that cheered me somewhat.

The stunning woman who sat next to Victor had her hand on his shoulder. She shook out her long glossy black hair, flipping it out of her face. My eyes met her amber-colored ones and she dipped her head in acknowledgment, straight-faced, before looking away again.

As I continued walking closer, my eyes were drawn to the girl sitting in the next chair over, pulled by the force of her unwavering stare. She appeared to be in her mid-teens, and I guessed she was the woman's daughter. The two looked very much alike. The noticeable differences were that the girl had a fairer complexion and her eyes were an arresting shade of blue. These she leveled at me without so much as blinking. Uncomfortable under her scrutiny, I looked away to the next person at the table.

Beside the girl was a younger boy. He also had fair skin, blue eyes, and black hair, only his topped his head with a riot of curls. He was also staring at me, but with a look that was much more wide-eyed and guileless than the girl's. When I caught him looking, his face dropped and his cheeks flamed.

My pace had slowed as I drew up to the table. Across from Victor, the only one sitting on the side I approached from, was a man who looked to be in his late twenties. He had short sideburns, but his was face clean shaven. The color of his hair was a paler version of Victor and Cassandra's, a golden-red. This man wore his button-down shirt untucked over khaki slacks. He sat leaning forward, arms crossed on the table. The look he sent my way at first was irrefutably a smirk, but then his gaze drifted lower and I instinctually crossed my arms over my chest. Next to this man were two empty place settings. I faltered momentarily, but then lowered myself into the seat I came to first, leaving a vacant spot between me and the man. I heard him chuckle. I cursed myself inwardly for advertising my apprehension so openly. Surely people who leave an open seat get torn to shreds by black bears.

"Miss Cassidy, it is with pleasure I would like to extend my most sincere thanks for joining us here at Willow Glen," the man at the head of the table announced. His voice carried loud and clear, but his deep intake of breath before speaking, and with each subsequent sentence, suggested that he was drawing on his energy reserves to make it so. "Allow me to make introductions. I am Nathaniel Dorn, the patriarch of this little clan. I believe you are already acquainted with my eldest son, Victor. Next to him is his lovely wife, Zahira, and their children, Evelyn and Julian. On your side of the table there is my other son, Jameson." Here Nathaniel paused to glare at the empty place setting between his second son and myself. "Deborah!" he bellowed, but with an unmistakable tremor in his voice. A stout woman I would later learn was the housekeeper hastened into the room.

"Sir?" she responded, hands clenched together in front of a thick waist.

"I thought I gave explicit instructions that Cassandra was to join us for dinner this evening."

Deborah bobbed her head, not meeting her employer's eyes. "You did, Sir. I tried my best to persuade her. But she refused, Sir."

Victor's fist pounded against the table and I jumped in my seat. He brushed his wife's hand from his shoulder and pushed himself to standing. "I will remind her that she does not have the luxury of refusing," he declared, turning from the table.

"Wait!" Nathaniel demanded, raising a hand. His shoulders lifted and then fell as he released a great, wheezing sigh. "Leave her. It's no matter." He turned toward me again. "Cassandra always was a willful child," he explained.

Victor remained standing. "The problem is she is no longer a child. And continuing to treat her as such is only going to create even more trouble for this family than it already has."

Nathaniel glowered at his son. "Victor. I said leave her."

Victor's face had assumed an unattractive purple tint. Nevertheless, he dropped back into his chair.

Nathaniel cleared his throat and then lifted a fist to his mouth as it transformed into a fit of coughing. When he had regained control, he addressed me once more. His voice had lost some of its fervor. "I apologize, Miss Cassidy. I hope you can forgive us. My family doesn't always see eye to eye on some subjects. I do hope you can overlook this, and find your stay here a most comfortable one."

I decided that if Nathaniel Dorn were going to act as if this were a run-of-the-mill social visit, it would behoove me to do the same. "It's a pleasure to meet you all. Thank you for welcoming me into your home."

The man sitting two places down from me, the one who had been introduced as Jameson, snorted into his glass of water. Victor and his wife exchanged an indecipherable look.

Just then the woman Deborah bustled back into the room bearing a tray of dishes. She began to serve us dinner. The meal was delivered in courses, and we were presented first with salads and steaming bowls of soup.

"Tell me, Miss Cassidy," Nathaniel said as he churned his soup with a spoon. "What areas of nursing are you skilled in?"

"I got a job in maternity right after graduating from nursing school," I answered. "Since then I've only ever done labor, delivery, and postpartum care."

"And apparently she also makes house calls," Victor interjected.

I turned to Victor, flashed him my most dazzling smile. "Yes, that's true," I bit out. "Obviously." I knew I had to be cautious around these people, but being backed into a corner has always made my own hackles rise.

Nathaniel reached a hand up and stroked his chin. I noticed that he hadn't actually eaten any of the soup he had been toying with. "I see. And do you recall, back in nursing school, having any experience with patients who felt short of breath or suffered fainting spells? Perhaps bringing up blood when they coughed?"

Victor shifted in his seat and spoke up again. "Father, surely our guest of honor does not wish to discuss such things at the dinner table. Let us speak of something else."

"Hmm." Nathaniel nodded in acquiescence. An uncomfortable silence fell over the room as most people concentrated on their meals. Several times I looked up to see the girl Evelyn watching me and making no effort to hide it. Her brother was slurping noisily at his soup. Deborah soon entered with the next course.

Jameson eventually broke the silence. "Zahira, I hear you spoke with your family today. Tell us, how is your cousin faring after his little mishap?"

Zahira pursed her lips as she lifted smoldering eyes to her brother-in-law. "Your concern is touching," she said in a voice that suggested that it was anything but. "We remain hopeful that he will make a full recovery. A talented young man such as himself doesn't deserve what happened to him." She shook her head and speared another bite of food.

"It was his own foolishness that got him into that mess," Nathaniel asserted, his demeanor strengthened by vehemence.

"I will thank you not to call my cousin a fool, Nathaniel," Zahira replied.

"What else does one call someone who has been blessed with gifts the rest of the world only dreams of, and yet puts himself in harm's way in an attempt to seize even more?" Nathaniel countered. I looked first one way, then the other, trying to follow the exchange.

"One might call that person a *greedy bastard*," Jameson offered in answer.

Victor piped up. "Or simply power-hungry."

"Ha!" Jameson exclaimed. "What color is the kettle?"

"Alright, alright. That's enough of that," Nathaniel declared, and then instantly erupted into another outburst of coughing. He held his linen napkin in front of his face until the fit had subsided. "Let us stop bickering so in front of our guest. She does not need to hear our petty squabbles."

Jameson twisted in his seat and threw an arm over the back of the empty chair between us.

"My father is right, of course. We shouldn't bore you with such things. Please, Miss Cassidy-Anna, isn't it?-tell us what neurotic tendencies *your* family has."

I smiled uncertainly. I didn't think an actual answer was expected of me. Nathaniel gave another loud sigh, and the others across the table were back to focusing on their food. I resumed picking at my own dinner, trying to manage to get some of it down despite the knots in my belly.

The fact that I could sense Jameson still watching me didn't help matters.

This time the quiet was not nearly as painful, since I had discovered what the alternative was like.

After a time, Deborah padded back into the room to begin clearing the dishes. "Well," Nathaniel said, dabbing at his face with his napkin. "In this house it is customary to enjoy a *digestif* in the drawing room after dinner. Or for those who prefer not to drink, or are too young," here the boy Julian let out a grunt of exasperation, "at least to come visit with the rest of the family. I would be honored if you would join us, Miss Cassidy." Feeling like I had little choice, I agreed.

I followed the others to where the drawing room was located just down the hall. The room looked like a larger version of the parlor I had been in the day before. In addition to a long couch in the center and various armchairs and end tables, there stood an expansive liquor cabinet, a writing desk, and a set of shelves displaying an assortment of curios. Frederick was in the room dusting as we arrived. "Ah, brandy time, is it, Sirs? Shall I serve you?" he inquired.

"That won't be necessary, Frederick," Victor answered as he strolled over to the liquor cabinet. "I'm sure you've done quite enough today as it is. I think I can handle the pouring."

"How very considerate of you, Brother," Jameson commented as he settled himself in front of another empty fireplace, one arm braced against the mantel. Frederick bowed and retreated from the room, while Victor began preparing the drinks.

"Usually we drink brandy," Nathaniel explained to me as he lowered himself into an armchair with a groan. "But if that isn't to your taste, you might prefer sherry."

"Of course, that would mean opening a new bottle," Victor interjected, "when we have a perfectly good cognac all ready to go here."

Nathaniel *harumphed*. "The choice is yours, dear. Opening a bottle of sherry would certainly be no trouble at all."

Despite how tempted I was to put Victor out of his way for my sake, I didn't want to place myself any further on his bad side than I already was. "The brandy will be fine," I answered. I wasn't usually much for alcohol, but I didn't want to come off as rude. Besides, if ever there was a time to give myself over to the drink, to blunt my physical senses, this seemed like it. I had been coerced into a less than ideal situation; an anesthetizing sort of apathy might be just the thing I needed to see me through the remainder of the evening. On the other hand, there was the chance that liquor might loosen my tongue instead, giving me reign to spout off how I really felt about the circumstances without regard to the consequences, potentially dire as they were.

Evelyn came up behind her father and reached for one of the crystal tumblers of amber liquid he had poured. Turning, she swished the glass around and then carried it over to where Nathaniel sat. "Here you are, Grandfather dear," she said, extending the glass to him.

Nathaniel patted his granddaughter's hand. "Thank you, love."

Victor dispensed the other tumblers around the room. I held mine up, gave it a cautious sniff. "You have beautiful children," I said to Zahira, attempting to make small talk. "They're very well mannered."

In between sips of her drink Zahira rolled her eyes to the ceiling. "Indeed, but children can be so *trying* at times. If it weren't for passing on one's genes, I'd say the little monsters were hardly worth the trouble!" she retorted, poking her elbow playfully at her son where he perched on the arm of her chair.

"A fact my father has recently been forced to face," Victor added.

I wasn't sure how to respond to either of those comments, so I focused instead on the glass in my hand. I brought it to my lips and tipped it up, taking a tentative sip. Not terrible, but certainly something that was going to take some getting used to.

Nathaniel seemed to have withdrawn into himself as he sloshed his brandy around in its glass and stared at it in between swigs, sighing occasionally. No one spoke for a while. If this was how the Dorn family visited with one another, no wonder Cassandra had not cared to participate.

I nursed my own drink. As everyone else finished the last dregs of their spirits I noted self-consciously that more than half of mine remained.

"You going to finish that?" I heard someone murmur into my ear. With the words came a rush of warmth against my neck, breath carrying currents of a spicy vanilla scent from the cognac. Half turning in my seat, I saw that Jameson had left his post at the fireplace and stood bent at the waist behind my chair. I happily surrendered my glass to him. Jameson tossed it back, draining the liquor within seconds. Watching his Adam's apple bob up and down as he swallowed made my own throat burn in sympathy.

Nathaniel returned to his senses at last. "I am afraid we are not the most pleasant company of late, Miss Cassidy. Our family has been experiencing quite a difficult time recently."

"Oh, you've all been lovely," I lied.

"I invite you to spend the rest of your evening exploring the house and familiarizing yourself with your new surroundings. We have quite an impressive library, if you are interested in such things. I'm afraid you'll find much of the house not in use these days, there being so few of us living here at the moment. Those rooms have been closed off for the time being." He clapped his hands against the tops of his thighs. "And now, if you don't mind, this old man shall retire."

That seemed to be the cue everyone had been waiting for. The family left their seats and began to file out of the room. The empty glasses were left sitting around on the tables in the room; presumably cleaning them up was something that was still left to the butler. Nathaniel hung back, gesturing that I should exit before him.

Well, that ordeal was over. I had come out on the other side of my first evening with the Dorns relatively unscathed. With a sense of relief, I followed the others out of the room.

3

July 25th, 2013

After writing yesterday's journal entry I decided to keep tradition alive and have a drink in the drawing room, even if I was all alone. In fact, I rather felt like getting myself drunk. All I was missing was a sympathetic bartender, wiping up rings of condensation with a worn cloth while offering an ear for my tale of woe.

I know, self-pity is never an attractive characteristic. As it was, I didn't get very far with my endeavor. At first a thrill overtook me as I flung open the glass doors to the liquor cabinet and considered its contents. I decided the brandy was my best bet considering my goal, but popped open the fresh bottle of sherry anyway, simply out of spite. *Take that, Dorn family!*

I was never very good at being a rebel.

I poured the cognac into a tumbler, reveling at the drops that splashed onto the carpet. "Down the hatch," I said to no one. Bracing myself, I threw my head back and emptied that sucker. I was glad there was no one there to see the awful face I'm sure I made.

On second thought, I decided that maybe I would switch to the sherry. After taking a minute to recover, I refilled my glass. I would take this one a little slower.

After a couple of sips I heard an inquisitive meow from below. I looked to see Dinah watching me, her tail curled in the air behind her. When I first arrived at Willow Glen I kept her confined to my rooms. Now I let her have the run of the place.

"I know," I said, meeting those round yellow eyes. "This is pretty sad, right?" Dinah just stared.

Admitting defeat, I smacked my glass down onto one of the tables. Reconsidering, I picked it back up again. I would bring it to the kitchen and rinse it out before heading back up to the room. After all, if I didn't clean it up, who would?

"Come on, girl," I called back to Dinah, "let's go to bed." She trailed after me on dainty paws, happy of the company.

After leaving the drawing room that first evening at Willow Glen I felt mentally drained, but physically I was too keyed up to settle down for the night. I followed Nathaniel's suggestion of exploring the place. Even the halls themselves were a sight to be seen; niches set within the walls displayed ornately painted vases and busts of apparently notable personages. Most of these were men, but there were some women, too. The names on the plaques were none that I recognized. The wainscoting throughout the home was anything but simple, covered with delicate friezes. No matter what I might think of its inhabitants, the house itself was magnificent. With all the stopping and gaping I did, it took a while for me to cover any sort of distance.

I did encounter some locked doors along the way, as Nathaniel had forewarned, but eventually I came across the library. I have always loved books, and my heart nearly fell still at the sight of two tiers of bookshelves all along each wall of the room. A narrow winding staircase led to the upper level. Sconces located on both levels bathed the expansive space in a diffuse light. A broad mahogany table dominated one end of the room, an overstuffed sofa and chairs arranged at the other.

The library was suffused with a silence that I found comforting. Advancing into the room, I approached one wall of leather-bound books. I grazed a finger across the spine of the first volume and traced a line down to the last on the shelf. That one I pulled out from its place to inspect. Gold leaf lettering on the front identified it as *The Origin of Species* by Charles Darwin.

"Looking for a bit of light reading?"

"Oh!" I jerked in surprise and spun around at the same time, a combination of moves that sent the book spinning through the air. It landed several feet in front of me with a resounding *thud.*

It was Jameson who had spoken. He must have come into the room without my noticing. He stood with hands slid into his pants pockets, thumbs hooked over the edges, staring at where Darwin's masterpiece lay awry on the floor. With copper brows raised, he lifted his eyes, green and penetrating, to consider me through fine lashes.

"Oh," I repeated. "It's you." Still, my heart continued to race. I was annoyed. Couldn't he have given some warning before startling me like that? Did he always look so smug? Like he knew just what reaction the sight of him standing there like that had on me, and he was enjoying my discomfort? I was tempted to give him a piece of my mind. I bit my tongue, though. Jameson Dorn made me nervous, even if in an entirely different way than his brother did.

He flashed me a grin that appeared much more sincere than any Victor had ever given me. "You're right! It *is* me!" He sauntered over to the table and swung a chair around. Straddling the seat, he sat in it backwards, arms crossed atop the back of the chair. "But for future reference, you can call me Jameson. Everybody does. Well, most everybody. I can think of a few people who have some other choice names for me." His face held a slight flush. He seemed relaxed, amiable, and quite possibly inebriated.

I scurried forward and bent down to retrieve the fallen book. Remembering the appraising looks he had given me at dinner, I sprung back up and clutched the book in front of my chest, shielding myself. "Did you follow me in here?" I asked.

Jameson shrugged. "I have to admit, I find watching you amusing."

I felt my own cheeks begin to glow. Turning around, I stepped back to the shelf and slid Darwin's book back in its place. "I didn't realize my life was a spectator sport," I retorted. I turned to face Jameson again and placed my hands on my hips, then remembered myself and crossed my arms in front of my chest once more. Jameson's smile widened, and I felt myself grow more aggravated. "Well you could help me out by cluing me in on what the hell is going on here, instead of letting me stumble through it all on my own. Unless, of course, that would ruin your fun."

His face softened. "I am in a generous mood this evening. No doubt due in small part to drinking your brandy as well as my own." He extended his arms and held them outstretched over the back of the chair, palms up. "Ask me whatever it is you might want to know."

I took a cautious step forward. "Okay." Where to start? "So tell me what the deal is with your sister and her baby."

"The deal? Well that is quite a broad inquiry. But given what I heard happened at the hospital, I think I see what you'd really like to know." He crossed his arms once again. "Cassandra and her baby are unharmed. My father has ordered that they be confined to her room. It's more like a suite of rooms, actually, at the back of the house. Cozy, nice view."

I was puzzled, but relieved. While being imprisoned by your own family is hardly an ideal situation, I had feared much worse for Cassandra and her baby.

"She was so scared," I explained to Jameson. "I even thought their lives might be in danger. His, or hers. Or both."

"They were," he replied. "By all rights they should both be confined to their coffins in our charming family graveyard right now, rather than in the house. But Cassandra has always been my father's favorite. He could not bring himself to sentence her to death, and he was helpless to ignore her pleas for the life of her child. Internment within her rooms is a far less dreadful punishment, I think you'll agree."

My mouth opened and shut a couple of times before I could muster a response. "Punishment for *what*?"

Jameson held my gaze. His grin had dwindled to a mere crook of the lips, and some of the mischievous shine had fled his eyes. "For conceiving a child with a human," he answered finally.

I think my mind might have frozen at that time. Synapses ceased firing. Was he messing with me? Was this just another form of cruelty? If this was a joke, I didn't get it. "So you're saying your sister isn't human?"

"I'm saying none of us in this family are."

I wondered if this was just more of his teasing. I wasn't sure if I should be indignant or intrigued. The uncertainty wound up causing me to just feel rather annoyed. "Okay. I'll play along. If you're not human, then what are you?" I asked.

"You mean besides handsome, intelligent and witty?" His attempt at humor was half-hearted, more like a reflex. In actuality he seemed to be preparing to enter more serious territory. He shifted in his seat. "We call ourselves the Sentient. Some self-important old fool devised that name ages ago. We know things. Powerful things. Things the rest of humanity never figured out." He suddenly pushed himself to standing and crossed to another of the library's walls. "Certain knowledge allowed us to alter ourselves, to develop abilities that could be passed on genetically to offspring. For that reason the aforementioned old fools like to think of us as a new race, a separate species other than mere humans. But of course by definition two species can't breed and create viable offspring. So my sister has done her part to disprove that theory." I had twisted in my place to follow his progress through the room. Having found the book he had been after, he lifted it off the shelf and carried it back to the table. "Here. This details some of our humble beginnings."

I slid into a seat and studied the book. "*A History of Alchemy*?" I said, flipping open the cover. As I skimmed through the pages I paused every once in a while to read a passage:

"...with the goal of evolving from a diseased and transient state into a healthy and everlasting one..."

"...transforming base materials into gold as an analogy for personal purification..."

"...achieving perfection, which for humankind would mean longevity, proceeding to immortality, and, finally, redemption..."

Jameson had been reading over my shoulder. He grunted and said, "Well, we have quite a way to go for the perfection and redemption bits, as you probably can see for yourself after having met my delightful relations."

"But the rest of it?"

"The longevity we've mastered, by managing to slow the aging process. We usually live approximately twice as long as the normal human life span, give or take a couple of decades. We've made some small progress on the immortality front. Which is precisely why my father's illness is so distressing. The other Sentient would be rather alarmed, if they knew. Panicked, even."

"What, none of you has gotten sick before?" I asked, scanning the book's many cryptic symbols and diagrams.

Out of the corner of my eye I saw Jameson shake his head. "No. We can die from physical trauma, if the damage is extensive enough. Murder is not unheard of in our ranks. But we are immune to illness. Long ago our forefathers discovered how to fortify our bodies against such things. My father's condition is unprecedented, and thus, very worrisome." I realized I was shaking my head while he spoke. I clapped the book shut.

"Having trouble believing me?" Jameson wanted to know.

"Well, yes, actually. Can you give me any proof?"

"Stick around for another century or so you'll find me still alive and well. A handsome, intelligent and witty middle-aged man. Unless of course you mean to murder me before then."

I must have looked nonplussed. With a brusque nod of his head, he took a few steps backward and beckoned for me to follow him. "Let me show you something." He strode to the opposite end of the library, near the lounge area. When he saw that I sat rooted to my chair the smirk crept back onto his face. "We may not be human, but I assure you we are not vampires either. I promise I won't bite you. Not unless you ask me to."

The way he looked at me was so intense it was like his piercing gaze fixed me to the spot, caught up in his scrutiny. I felt like I was the only thing in the room, the only thing truly present, and everything else faded into the background. It was a feeling I was not used to. It made my insides turn to slush and I had to fight the urge to find a place to hide myself away from his notice. Instead I collected myself enough to rise from my chair and cross to where Jameson stood waiting for me, making a conscious effort to keep my head held high, to not give away the quivering I felt in my belly.

"You see this here?" He indicated a small design that had been etched into the wood paneling of the wall between two sets of bookshelves. It looked like a spear, or maybe an arrow, at an angle pointing up and to the right. A wavy line wound along the shaft. I watched as Jameson placed a hand flat over the design and a muted light emanated from the spot he touched, shining between his fingers. A great rumbling noise filled the room, taking me by surprise. I was disoriented for a moment, the room seemed to move around me. And then I realized it *was* moving. The bookshelf to the right of the symbol was slowly swinging outward. It was opening just like a door.

I could do nothing but watch until the shelf finally came to a rest and all was quiet once more. Through the opening that had materialized I could see what seemed to be another library. This one had walls of stone, and more modest bookshelves. Even from a distance I could tell the books they held were much older than those in the outer-library. I was overcome with the musty scent of knowledge waiting to be soaked up. It brought to mind the image of brittle pages crumbling beneath the brush of a finger.

Near the center of the room a pedestal held up a massive book. I took a step forward to get a closer look, but Jameson flung an arm out in front of me. A tingling warmth flared where his arm pressed against my ribs. I leapt back as if I had been stung. Even after the contact was broken, I swear I could still feel the heat of his touch.

"Sorry," he said, "you can look but you can't enter. The others would probably be furious if they knew I even showed you this much." He didn't seem at all displeased by that idea. He placed a hand on the wall once more and the bookshelf began to slide shut. It slammed into place with a final scraping sound. "Now, you try."

I looked to Jameson, who gestured toward the wall with his chin. I laid a tentative hand over the symbol, just as he had. Nothing happened.

"You see, these things only work for those with Sentient blood in their veins." I let my hand fall.

"Alright. Okay." I turned toward Jameson. "So you and your family are part of a group of people called the Sentient. You know all sorts of really important stuff. You live a super long time. You hide libraries. But none of this explains why Cassandra is being punished for having a baby with a human?"

"How neglectful of me." Jameson began walking back toward the other end of the room and I followed a few steps behind. "We have a prophecy. Because what new race of enlightened beings wouldn't quake in the face of superstition and call it divination?

"Long ago it was foretold that the offspring of a Sentient and a human would be born. This half-breed would have the ability to destroy the Sentient and everything we stand for, unravel the very soul of our being, et cetera, et cetera–you know, cryptic prophecy language. In response, any time an ill-fated Sentient made the mistake of impregnating or becoming impregnated by a human, the lords of the families would have the child, and usually the offenders, executed. They do not take kindly to the threat of having the very souls of their beings unraveled.

"That is why Cassandra and her whelp were supposed to have been killed. But, as we have already established, my father could not bear it and sentenced them to indefinite confinement instead. If the other Houses ever discovered the truth – well, let's just say the proverbial shit would hit the fan. The proverbial fan, I suppose."

I considered all of this information. After a while, I asked, "Then why would any Sentient ever...you know, why would you ever sleep with a human?"

Jameson slid his hands back into his pockets. "Why did Juliet bat her eyes at Romeo? Why did Lancelot make off with his king's wife? Maybe for some just the idea of forbidden love is enough." He shrugged. "Besides, not all of us are thrilled with what the Sentient have come to stand for. An inflated sense of entitlement can be a very unattractive thing. A dangerous thing."

Jameson had certainly been forthcoming. I was getting answers, even if they were far from what I had expected. But something was making me uneasy. Why would he be sharing all of this with me so freely? I could think of at least one possible answer.

Perhaps the Dorn family was going to ensure that I could never pass it on.

I asked anyway. "Aren't you afraid that I'll reveal all your secrets to the rest of the world?"

"What I have told you this evening, sweetheart, is hardly all of our secrets. Besides, I don't see you as a threat."

I felt a bitter chill suffuse the marrow of my bones and a shudder raced through me. "Why not?"

Jameson looked me up and down unhurriedly before he answered. "Too short." With that, he left the library.

4

July 26th, 2013

I had been reading a novel I took from the library when I glanced up and noticed Dinah at the end of the bed. She had been in the middle of a very meticulous self-cleaning when her head snapped up. She froze, a hind leg held stiff in the air. Her eyes were fixed on the door to the hall, immense yellow globes with pupils shrunk to pinpricks. I waited, watching, but still she didn't move. Goosebumps sprung up all over my skin.

I eased myself off of the bed and tip-toed to the door. I paused to listen. There was only silence. Fortifying myself with a deep breath, I turned the handle. In one sudden motion I thrust the door open and leaned out into the hallway.

What did I expect to find lurking there? I can't say for sure, but the emptiness that greeted me was just as chilling as anything I could have imagined. I looked back at Dinah and saw that she was now tucked up against a mound of sheets and resting her chin on her front paws, eyes squeezed shut.

Feeling more than half a fool, I drew back and pulled the door shut. It was then I decided that it was time to continue working on my story, to keep my mind from drifting off to perilous places. These days I do enough fruitless musing as it is.

I woke the next morning to someone knocking at my door. I shuffled over and opened it to see Deborah. "Good morning, Miss," the housekeeper greeted me. "I was sent to inform you that Master Nathaniel wishes for you to go to him in his chambers in an hour's time." I thanked her. She smiled and bobbed her head before hurrying away.

I showered and dressed. Wondering what time it was, I picked up my cell phone, but the thing had already died. I dropped it back onto the desk, resigned to the fact that my life seemed to have become an unending string of unfortunate incidents. With the loss of that last lifeline to the normal world, the nerves began jittering around inside my stomach. I did my best to tamp them back down. There was nothing for it but to forge ahead with the task I had been set, no matter how crazy it might be. I had come back willingly to Willow Glen in the hope that I might do some good, that there were people I could help. People who needed me. Steeling myself, I prepared to press on and have a more thorough look at my prospective patient.

The medical supplies I had brought from home included a stethoscope, blood pressure cuff and the like. I gathered these to my chest and turned for the door. Dinah had jumped down from the bed when I was readying myself and was crunching at her food dish. I stooped down to run my hand over her silky back. "Wish me luck," I whispered to her, then left for my appointment with Nathaniel.

Once in the hall I realized I didn't know where to find Nathaniel's room. I looked up and down the corridor, not sure which way to proceed.

It was then I heard the noise, a hollow-sounding *smack*. A moment later it came again. It sounded as though it were coming from my right, so I decided to start walking toward the source; it was as good a way as any. Following the sound led me into an adjoining hallway.

Several yards down I saw the boy, Julian, bouncing a red rubber ball off of the wall. He would thrust the ball against the ornately patterned red and gold wallpaper, after which it would next strike the floor and leap back up to his waiting arms.

"Good morning!" I called out as I approached along the carpet runner that passed down the center of the hallway. I was going for cheerful, doing my best to sound as if this was a normal morning like any other for me, but I must have taken the boy by surprise. He swung around to face me and let the ball bound away across the floor. He gave me the same wide-eyed stare he had the night before, mouth hanging slightly open.

"I'm sorry," I said, pulling up short. "I didn't mean to startle you. I was just wondering if you could tell me how to get to your grandfather's room?"

Julian snapped his mouth shut and swallowed. He pivoted on his heel and began scampering away. At first I was afraid I had scared him off, but when he reached the end of the hall he turned back to me and pointed toward his right. I hurried over to him, tucking my equipment under one arm and bending down to scoop up the red ball on the way.

"The double doors at the end of the hall," Julian said, his voice just above a whisper.

"Thank you." I held the ball out in the palm of my hand. He snatched it up and went on staring. I was actually feeling bad about how uncomfortable I seemed to make him. Flashing him a quick smile, I left him and walked in the direction he had indicated.

Soon I was knocking on the double doors. I didn't hear any response, so I knocked again, this time with more force. Still nothing. I eased the door open and called out, "Mr. Dorn?" Not receiving an answer, I slipped inside the room. My heartbeat quickened; I felt like a criminal sneaking in, but no matter how tempting it was to steal back to my own room, my instructions had been pretty clear. "Nathaniel?" I tried again, louder.

I had stepped into a sitting area of sorts. It was decorated in much the same fashion as the rest of the house. Here also there was a mauve divan arranged in one corner and crystal beads dangling from the lampshades. The main focal piece of the room was a large portrait adorning one of the walls, showing a woman with auburn hair in a plum-colored gown. Eyes crinkling as she smiled with benevolence, the woman posing for the portrait appeared to be middle-aged. Peering closer I could make out the words inscribed on the frame's plaque: *Vivienne Cotillard Dorn, 1942, Dorn House, Mechelen.*

Dragging my eyes from the portrait, I noticed to my left an archway through which there loomed an immense four poster bed, and to my right the entrance to a private bath. It seemed Nathaniel had a suite of rooms. Straight ahead, sliding glass doors opened onto a balcony. I felt a warm breeze sweep across my arms, and saw that the door to the balcony stood open a crack. Lured by the fresh air, I slid the glass open further and stepped outside.

The view from where I stood was breathtaking. Not only could I see the tree-covered hills sloping away from the estate, but also the lavish formal gardens that I hadn't yet realized existed behind the house. Vivid colors sprouted in an impressive array below me. Here and there marble statuary thrust up amidst the plant life. At the far end I could make out a pond and a gazebo poking through the greenery. I caught sight of a gardener toiling by a massive shed.

"Beautiful, isn't it?"

The voice came from by my elbow and caught me completely unawares. "Holy shit!" I couldn't help exclaiming. My hand flew to my throat. As absorbed as I had been with the view, I hadn't even noticed Nathaniel himself reclining in a lounge chair out on the balcony. A tray laden with breakfast food sat on the glass-topped table next to him.

"Yes, I suppose that's another way of saying it," he quipped.

I thought of how it must look, me letting myself into his rooms and enjoying the sights from his balcony without even knowing he was there. "Oh, I am so sorry! There was no answer when I knocked, so-"

Nathaniel chuckled and held up a placatory hand. "Relax, Miss Cassidy. I was expecting you. If I did not mean for you to be here, you would never have reached me."

"It *is* gorgeous here," I said, trying to draw his attention away from my embarrassment.

"Yes," Nathaniel agreed. "This was always Vivienne's favorite place to stay. We have other estates, you see. A handful of them spread around the globe. But Vivienne loved it here best." He fell silent, prey to memories.

"Vivienne?" I prompted.

"My wife," he explained, returning his attention to me. "My beloved wife. You may have noticed her portrait hanging back there." He gestured with his thumb to the sitting room behind us.

I nodded, immediately recognizing the resemblance between the woman in the painting and Cassandra. "Your wife, she's..."

"Deceased," Nathaniel confirmed. He rubbed at his chest, eyes fixed somewhere far beyond Willow Glen Manor. "Going on ten years now." Another moment of silence passed before he tore his eyes from the past and leveled them back at me. His lips twitched. "But this is not what you came to hear. Forgive an old man for a roaming mind."

"Of course." I cleared my throat and pulled my equipment out from under my arm. "I hear you haven't been feeling well lately?"

"Quite right. And I believe my son has explained to you the unusual circumstances surrounding my case."

I faltered. How much of what I had been told did he know? What exactly was he referring to? I didn't know if he just meant what Victor had said about how he rarely fell ill and seldom left the house. Or was he aware of everything Jameson had revealed to me the night before in the library?

Nathaniel noticed my hesitation. "About the Sentient?" he offered.

"Oh. Yes."

Nathaniel nodded, his countenance grim. He reached for the glass of orange juice on the table by his side and emptied it, then set it back on the tray with a sigh of satisfaction. His food, on the other hand, remained scarcely touched. "Remove this, would you, Miss Cassidy? Just put it on the table in the sitting room and Deborah will collect it later. Thank you."

I cast around for a place to put my gear and ended up setting it down on the seat of one of the other chairs. I lifted the breakfast tray from the table, but didn't move away. "Listen-do you mind if I call you Nathaniel? You want me here as your nurse, right? Then I have to tell you, the protein in these eggs might help you keep your strength up."

He waved a dismissive hand through the air. "I've had enough. I hardly even have the energy to eat these days. Too much damn effort."

I brought the food tray to the sitting room, then returned to the balcony and picked up my stethoscope. "So can you tell me what's been going on?"

"I have been feeling rather weak as of late. I have difficulty sleeping. Sometimes I overexert myself and then feel as though I will lose consciousness." I gestured at Nathaniel's chest with my stethoscope and he nodded his consent. Sliding the end under the collar of his shirt, I took a moment to listen to his lungs. His breath sounds were clear, his respiratory rate was within the normal range, although at the higher end. His heart tones were strong, but the rate was definitely too fast.

"Were you doing anything physical recently?" I asked.

"I have been sitting out here since waking."

I wrapped the blood pressure cuff around his upper arm. The reading I obtained was a bit on the low side, but still acceptable.

After removing the cuff I lifted one of Nathaniel's hands in my own and pinched a fingertip, blanching it, and watching to see how long it took for the color to return. I knelt down in front of him. "Would it be alright for me to take a look at your feet?"

"Whatever you think is necessary."

I removed his slippers of woven leather and touched my fingertips to the top of each foot. They did appear somewhat swollen, puffed out along the surface, but I was able to discern his pulses without much trouble.

His feet were normal in color. I covered them up again, and pushed myself back up to standing.

"Try to keep them elevated as much as you can throughout the day." I set my hands on my hips. "Now this next part might seem a little awkward, but if you're intent on keeping me here to help you get better, there are something personal things I'll need to keep track of."

"Please. My son apparently had no problem sharing plenty of private information with you last night. Anything you need to know, just ask," Nathaniel said.

I nodded. "Okay, then. I need to know how much you pee."

Nathaniel blinked. I mentally awarded myself a point for managing to shock a member of this smooth-talking family into speechlessness. "Trust me, I wouldn't be asking if it wasn't important. Do you think you could find something to store your urine in each time you go, until I have a chance to measure it? I need you to record how much you eat and drink each day, too."

Nathaniel shifted in his seat. "If you think it will help, then of course," he said, recovering his powers of speech.

We both turned at the sound of the main doors to his rooms opening. The housekeeper bustled in. She slammed a small silver key down onto the table near the entryway and smoothed unruly wisps of hair away from her face with both hands. "Sir, I apologize for the intrusion, but your daughter is still refusing to eat enough. I brought her a breakfast tray and she flat out told me to take it away without so much as looking at it! When I tried to insist, she threatened to hurl the tray against the wall if I didn't get it out of her sight immediately."

"My children can all be exceedingly stubborn, I'm afraid," Nathaniel said in my direction. Then, "She will eat when she is ready, Deborah."

The housekeeper grimaced and wrung her hands together. "If she doesn't starve herself to death first!" she blurted. She seemed embarrassed by her display of emotion in front of the master of the house, but it seemed to me that it stemmed from sincere concern for Cassandra.

With cheeks mottled, Deborah bobbed her head and made to leave the room.

"Oh, Deborah!" Nathaniel called after her. "See to it that a measuring device of some sort is brought up here, would you? You may leave it in the privy."

Deborah's brow furrowed in confusion, but her only response was to say, "Right away, Sir," before hurrying off to do as she was bid.

When the door clicked shut, I posed my next question. "Do you have a scale for weighing yourself around here?"

"I do," he answered. "That is in the privy as well."

"Great. From now on every day when you first get up in the morning I'd like you to weigh yourself and write it down."

"Very good," Nathaniel responded. Placing a limp hand to his brow he added, "I apologize for cutting this assessment short, Miss Cassidy, but I very much would like to lie down for a nap now."

Recognizing my dismissal, I gathered up my equipment once more, said goodbye, and crossed back into the sitting room. I was headed for the door when something caught my eye. The key Deborah had left on the table; presumably she had forgotten it in her haste to leave. If she had just come from Cassandra to complain about her refusal to eat, did that mean this was the key to her room?

I peeked over my shoulder and saw that Nathaniel's chin had already drooped down onto his chest. Apparently he had foregone the "lying down" part of his nap. The man really was sapped of all energy. Not taking the time to question the wisdom of it, I scooped the key up and stuffed it into my jeans pocket.

I backtracked through the corridors with a new spring in my step, motivated by the fear of getting caught in my act of insubordination. I couldn't shake the feeling that any Dorn who so much as looked at me would immediately know what I was up to. Thankfully Julian must have left to play somewhere else while I was with his grandfather. I made my way unseen to the back of the house.

My pace slowed when I spotted another set of double doors, which I presumed might lead to the suite where Cassandra was being held. Without much subtlety, I threw looks over both shoulders before approaching. My palm was sweaty when I reached into my pocket and pulled the key back out. I had all the reason in the world to defy these people who presumed to demand that I stay and do their bidding, but still I couldn't help feeling a twinge of guilt. It wasn't enough to stop me, however, and the key glided into the lock and turned with a satisfying *click.*

Easing one of the doors open revealed a set of rooms quite different from Nathaniel's. Instead of a separate space, a sitting area was included within the spacious bedroom itself, at the end opposite from a lacy canopy bed. The entire room itself was an oval shape. It was filled with fabrics in a gray and yellow damask pattern with accents of purple thrown in, the furnishings all white-washed. It looked like a page in a catalogue. A catalogue advertising things most people couldn't afford.

Off to the right of the main room was another private bath. The sitting area consisted of seats arranged around yet another fireplace. Against the far wall stood a crib and changing table. Over the top of the sofa I could see the back of a woman's bowed head. Suddenly feeling unsure of myself, I made my way warily over.

"Cassandra?" No answer. As I came around the side of the sofa, I saw she held the baby in her arms. He was asleep, little pink lips moving faintly in a suckling motion. Cassandra traced a gentle finger from his forehead down to the tip of his nose. Her face was somber.

I stood motionless. It was like a spell had settled over this room and I was in danger of breaking it with any swift movement.

Finally I had to say something. "Jameson told me. About what you are." I spoke softly.

"What we are," Cassandra murmured. So she hadn't been turned to stone after all. Still she kept her eyes on her son's face.

"What's his name?" I asked.

The first hint of a smile curled Cassandra's lips. "Wesley," she answered. She slipped her finger into one of the baby's tiny hands and he grasped onto it without waking.

I bent down and whispered, "Hello, Wesley." Straightening, I glanced around the room again. "Well, if you have to be held against your will somewhere, I guess this place isn't too shabby." I immediately regretted trying to make light of the situation, not sure how Cassandra would react.

"I call it my bower," she responded. "It has such a more pleasant ring to it than prison, don't you agree?"

Wesley began to squirm and let out a soft whimper. Cassandra discreetly put him to her breast. With his eyes still closed he began to nurse, one hand clinging to a strand of his mother's hair. I felt the anger begin to well inside of me again. How dare anyone try to interfere with such a natural bond as this? Life gifts you with someone you are inarguably meant to be with, and others threaten to rip that link apart. I fumed, but Cassandra was not the one my frustration was directed at, and so I made an effort to keep my voice gentle when I spoke.

"You know, if you're breastfeeding it really is important to make sure you're eating and drinking enough. You'll need plenty of fluids to maintain your supply of milk. And of course, Wesley needs you to pass on good nutrition." When I got no response, I returned to the previous subject. "Are you allowed to have visitors in here?"

"Jameson visits. Father prefers to pretend this whole situation doesn't exist. Victor and his wife are pompous prigs. I believe Victor thinks our father weak for not having us killed. My own brother." She choked on the last word. "And of course the servants come and go."

That reminded me of something that had occurred to me since moving in at Willow Glen. "I've only seen the butler, the housekeeper, and just today a gardener. It seems like a place this size would have more servants than that."

I noticed Cassandra's shoulders stiffen and worried that I'd frightened her off from talking anymore, but a moment later she offered me an explanation. "Our servants need to know about what we are, it becomes unavoidable. And the prevailing idea is that the fewer humans who know, the better."

And now I was one of the lucky few to be swept up into that category. The things I was learning at Willow Glen Manor were fascinating, to be sure, but still I worried about how my little cameo appearance in the lives of the Dorns was meant to end. Had the others here been forced into their servitude?

Speaking of humans in the Dorns' lives, I very much wanted to know about the man who had fathered Cassandra's baby, but of course it would have been in poor taste to ask. Especially since I didn't know what might have become of him.

Instead I said, "Listen, Cassandra, I'm sorry I wasn't able to help you back at the birth center. I didn't realize...I didn't know."

Cassandra began shaking her head vigorously and I saw her eyes well up with tears. "No, I am the one who is sorry. I should never have asked that of you. I was just so desperate. I never meant to get you mixed up in all of this."

There may have been truth in her words, but I certainly didn't blame Cassandra for how things had played out. My heart hurt for her. I felt compelled to place a hand on her shoulder. "It's alright. It doesn't matter. I'm here now."

"You are here now. And I am so very, very sorry."

It seemed Wesley had fallen back asleep while nursing. Cassandra shifted him back into her lap. We both watched his sleeping face for a time, mesmerized by the innocence and peace revealed there. A child so new to the world had no need to doubt his place in it. Or in this case perhaps he did, but mercifully he lacked the capacity to let this trouble him.

"I should probably go now," I said, rousing myself. "I don't think I'm supposed to be here." Cassandra only nodded. I started to make for the door when her voice stopped me. "Would you please tell Deborah I would take something to eat now?"

"Sure. Of course."

"And Anna? Lock the door again on your way out. I don't want any more trouble for you on my account."

As I left, I turned the little silver key in the lock again, feeling something like a monster as I walked away from where a woman and her baby remained prisoners in their own home. Although, to be fair, my circumstances were little better.

5

July 27th, 2013

I still have the book that Jameson showed me that first night in the library, *A History of Alchemy*. I've flipped through it a hundred times since then. I used to find the mystical diagrams and archaic symbols fascinating, enthralled as I poured over them trying to make meaning of the arcane markings. My heart would speed up with excitement each time I delved into those pages. Now I tear through them in my obsessive search for answers, getting angrier and more desperate each time I find none. At least, none that I can recognize.

One of the times I went through the book, something familiar caught my eye. It was an alchemical symbol that looked like an arrow with a curving line through it. The same design that marks the locations of the hidden entrances in Willow Glen Manor.

Yes, I said entrances, plural. There are more than just the one in the library. In fact, I discovered one right in this very room. There was a night not long ago when I was staring transfixed at the tapestry in my room, the one with the lady and the plant. I was thinking of the women of Willow Glen and their various troubles. There's myself, of course. And Cassandra, locked away for loving the wrong man. Vivienne, the late lady of the house. Not to mention the others...But I don't want to get ahead of myself.

It was while standing in front of the tapestry that I noticed the symbol engraved into the wall beside it. There was nothing I could do once I found it, I knew my meager human form would fail to activate whatever mechanism opens those disguised entrances. Whatever lies beyond the wall to my room is not for my eyes.

Besides the inner library, I've only ever seen inside one other of the secret rooms. But I'm sure there are plenty more I'll never find.

Anyway, the book explains that the meaning of the symbol is *purification*. I actually sneered when I read that.

I think, for better or for worse, some of Jameson may have rubbed off on me.

No one attempted to make small talk at dinner that evening, and yet it wound up being just as uncomfortable as it had been the night before. Both Victor and Jameson seemed to be in black moods, although I couldn't be sure why. Zahira and I took the hint not to try and draw them into conversation. Even the children must have sensed the brooding atmosphere and ate their food in silence. Nathaniel was directing every ounce of his attention toward taking tiny bites of his meal, and his brow shone with perspiration. Several times he tugged a handkerchief from his pocket and patted at his face.

For a while the only sounds filling the room were the clinking of silverware on dishes. When the meal drew to a close at last, Nathaniel spoke up.

"I'm afraid I don't feel up to our usual custom this evening. But please, I insist the rest of you continue to the drawing room without me."

"Are you quite sure?" Victor asked.

"I can help you to your seat, Grandfather," Evelyn offered.

Nathaniel gave a fervent shake of his head. "No, no. I want nothing so much as to go lie down. Go on, then."

We all obediently rose from our seats at the dinner table and trekked toward the drawing room. Once in the hallway and out of her grandfather's earshot, Evelyn spoke up. "Please, Father, may I have your permission to skip tonight?"

"Yeah," Julian echoed, "can we?"

"Yes, yes," Victor granted his blessing, shooing his children back down the corridor. It seemed this little ritual was usually for Nathaniel's benefit. The rest of us entered the drawing room and Victor set about preparing the drinks.

After passing out the glasses, he turned his attention to me. "So, Miss Cassidy, any insights yet on my father's affliction?"

I took a sip of brandy before answering. "Well it's been years since I've worked in regular adult care, but some of the signs and symptoms he's presenting with sound a lot like heart failure."

"Impossible."

I crooked an eyebrow. "Oh. Okay. Can I go home now, then?"

Victor narrowed his eyes at me. "If it were up to me you wouldn't even be here now. You should be thankful that my soft-hearted father is in charge around here and not me."

Anger swelled in my chest, pressing against my insides as it sought release. "Just how long do you people think you can keep me here?" I demanded to know.

It was Jameson who replied. "Well, we know there's no knight in shining armor ready to charge in here and rescue you from us evil bastards. And honestly, darling, you don't look the type able to save herself." I seethed as I watched him down the last of his brandy. Whatever dark cloud had been hovering over him at dinner seemed to have followed us to the drawing room, and I could almost feel the waves of aggravation radiating from his body. The promise of threats had hung over my head for days, but now I was downright insulted.

I wanted to get out of that room before I opened my mouth and got myself into any more trouble with those people. As much as I would have loved to punch someone, anyone, in the nose right at that moment, I balked at finding out how serious they were about the consequences of displeasing them. I slammed my glass on the table and muttered, "Thank you for the delightful company this evening," to no one in particular, and then walked out.

I decided that some fresh air would do me good. After meandering a bit I came across the kitchen, where Deborah was scrubbing dishes in a large double sink before slipping them into a dishwasher.

"Is there a back door to this place, or what?" I asked. Deborah lifted a soapy hand to point to a door off of the kitchen, just beyond where I stood. "Oh. Thanks." I wrenched the door open, tearing out into the clear nighttime air behind the manor house.

The chirping of crickets accompanied me as I crossed a terrace, trotted down some steps, and strode down the main path through the gardens. I came across a spot where the path split in four directions, with a fountain spouting in the center. I dropped down onto one of the benches that encircled the little crossroads. Pulling my legs up, I tucked my knees under my chin and wrapped my arms around them.

I tried to focus on my breathing in an effort to calm down. I knew I couldn't afford to anger these people. I had no problem picturing things getting ugly if I disappointed them. I rocked back and forth on the bench, willing myself to regain a measure of composure.

When the feelings of anger and frustration did begin to ebb, I was able to take in the sights around me. The shadowed foliage was bobbing in a gentle wind. The garden contained not only flowering shrubs and hedges, but also some trees scattered throughout. I realized the trees had lights hanging in them, sparkling white globes. I wasn't near enough to any of them to make out exactly what they were, but the effect was stunning. With the limbs of the trees swaying slightly in the breeze, I felt as though I were in some enchanted forest surrounded by will o' the wisps. I made a mental note not to follow those lights anywhere off the beaten path.

I heard the sound of a shoe scuffing gravel. Jameson walked into my line of sight and stopped in front of the fountain. He bent down and plucked a stone up from the ground.

"How did your mother die?" I asked him.

"Well, hello to you, too," he countered, twirling the stone around in his hand.

"Hi. How did your mother die? And when you answer, I'd appreciate it if you could keep any insulting barbs you're tempted to fling my way to yourself."

Jameson met my obstinate stare from beneath lowered lids. He blew out a long breath before responding. "It happened ten years ago. Every five years there are Sentient council meetings. Representatives from each of the most prominent Houses attend. They discuss advances in our research. A lot of politics. Most of them just like to hear themselves talk. Each time the location for the meeting is rotated from one family's residence to another. This particular meeting was to be held at the home of the Hakim family. Relatives of Zahira's.

"All of us traveled there, even Victor and Zahira's children. We wouldn't all sit for the actual meeting, but the gathering lasts for a few days and is treated like a celebration of sorts. It's one big party as much as anything; a chance for Sentient families to get together and let loose, such as it is." I could see his sneer even through the gloom, and hear it in his voice. Still he toyed with the stone in his hand. "The day after arriving, before the council meeting itself had even convened, my mother plummeted down the Hakims' stairs, breaking her neck along the way. A moment of inattention, a slip of the foot - these things simply don't happen with us. Through centuries of careful engineering our reflexes have become without equal. Right away everyone assumed foul play. My mother was pushed.

"As you might be able to imagine, things turned ugly after that. Everyone was pointing the finger at everybody else. The meeting was canceled, everybody returned home. We brought my mother back to bury her.

"At the next council meeting, five years ago, relations remained strained. Business was seen to, but everybody was on edge. I think the whole Sentient world breathed a sigh of relief when that week concluded and no one had died. Victor had wanted to turn the meeting into an inquisition, flush out the culprit to show the other families that the Dorns wouldn't sit meekly and accept such an insult. I think that's all our mother's death was to him: an insult. But my father didn't see the point of alienating all of the other families when we had no idea who was actually to blame. He spent those days trying to smooth things over, let the other families know they didn't need to walk on egg shells around us. He wanted to repair our relations with the other families and maintain our standing, whereas Victor wanted to assert ourselves over them. But in the end Victor has to abide by my father's word. Much to his perpetual consternation." I was still taking this all in when I realized Jameson was not going to say anymore.

"I'm sorry for your loss," I told him, sobered by his story.

"She was a remarkable woman," he said. "I think you would have liked her. She undoubtedly was the best of us. Her death struck my father the hardest. He and Victor express themselves differently, but that doesn't mean he wasn't angered by what had happened. He has never been quite the same since she died." He extended a hand toward me and I realized he was handing me the rock he had been fiddling with. I reached for it, wondering why on earth he would be giving me a rock.

I gasped when I saw what he dropped into my hand. No longer a dull gray stone, it had somehow been fashioned into a sparkling gemstone molded into the shape of a rose. Layers of petals lay unfurled in minute detail. The stone was as clear as the purest diamond. It still felt warm in my hand.

I looked up at Jameson, trying to wipe the look of astonishment from my face so that he wouldn't let it go to his head. "First you taunt me in front of your family. And then you expect me to accept flowers from you?"

He crooked his lips at me and shrugged. "I apologize for that. I have a reputation as an asshole to uphold, you see."

"I don't think you have to try very hard." I ran my thumb over the ridges of the petals. "But thank you anyway."

"Consider it a peace offering?"

"Hmm. For mocking me tonight, maybe. But for keeping me here against my will?"

The smile fell from his face. His voice dropped. "Convincing Victor to keep you on here rather than simply doing away with you was no easy feat for us." I swallowed hard, hearing my fears confirmed outright. Jameson's gaze dropped to my throat. "Contrary to what you might believe, Anna, I am trying to help you as best I can under the circumstances."

I was too shaken to reply. Jameson dipped his head at me in a parting gesture and strolled away, back toward the house. I shut my eyes and let my breath out in a rush.

I didn't stay out in the gardens for long after that. Opening my eyes again, I admired the way the twinkling lights reflected in the jewel I held cupped in my hand. Then I too went inside the house and to my room, and put forth my best effort to find sleep.

The next morning I returned to Nathaniel's rooms. I knocked and let myself in. Nathaniel was out on the balcony once again, and I experienced a moment of guilt ridden indecision. Sliding a hand into my pocket, I rubbed clammy fingertips over the smooth surface of the key I had lifted the day before. Should I try to slip it back where I had taken it from? Surely they must have already noticed it was missing, but maybe when they saw it on the table they would assume it had been there the whole time and was overlooked? Someone more practiced in deceit would have had no question about what to do, I'm sure, and pulled it off without a hitch. As it was, in one quick, jerky motion, I plunked the little key down and scurried away from it as swiftly as I could toward the balcony.

Before I had even reached the open glass doors, Nathaniel's voice came drifting in to me. "If you wished to see my daughter, all you had to do was ask." I stiffened. Did these people know *everything*? "You might as well keep the key. We have others. And I imagine it might do Cassandra some good to have company now and again."

I returned the key to my pocket, feeling sheepish. Apparently no one was worried that I might use the key to help Cassandra escape. Presumably they had other ways of ensuring she stayed put. I couldn't say I was surprised, not with the ideas floating through my mind of what these people might be capable of, but I was curious to know what those other means might be. I was fairly confident, however, that I was not the one to draw that sort of information from my hosts through nonchalant conversation. Deception was clearly not my forte.

In an effort to allow the awkwardness of the situation more time to dissipate before facing Nathaniel, I decided to check on things in the bathroom before joining him on the balcony. Right away I saw a tall clear plastic measuring cup sitting on the floor next to the toilet, filled partway with a dark amber fluid. Nathaniel was, at least, a compliant patient. Squatting to the floor, I wrinkled my nose and eyed the markings on the cup. There wasn't as much in there as I would have liked to see for a twenty-four hour period, but after running the numbers in my head I concluded that it was sufficient. Satisfied, I dumped the urine into the toilet and flushed it away. While washing my hands I saw a notebook of lined paper sitting by the sink. Nathaniel had written down his weight from earlier that morning.

Stepping out onto the balcony, I looked to Nathaniel's breakfast. Again it looked like most of it was still there.

"Another lovely day, isn't it?" Nathaniel remarked.

"It is." I could see the fountain and the circle of benches where I had sat the night before. The lights suspended in the trees had winked out in the daytime. The gardener was at work again.

"Another check-up, then?" Nathaniel asked. I nodded and repeated my assessment from the day before. Everything was essentially unchanged. His lips were pink and moist. I pinched the skin over the back of his hand to see that it retracted back to its normal position and didn't stay lifted.

"Any new symptoms?" I asked.

"Just this damnable headache."

"A headache? Any changes in your vision?"

"No, my dear."

"Okay, then. I think that's it for right now. Keep up with weighing yourself and collecting your urine. And make sure to try to drink enough fluids. Is there anything else you need from me before I go?"

Nathaniel began shaking his head, but stopped short. "Actually, there is. I would like your opinion on something. Do you see Tom down there, our gardener?"

I peeked back over the railing. "I see him."

"Is he an attractive man, would you say?"

The question took me by surprise. Where on earth was he going with this? I looked more carefully at the man wielding the gardening shears beneath us. I guessed he was probably in his mid-forties. He had a mop of blonde hair halfway to gray, and even from a distance his nose shone red. Either the man was suffering from an off-season cold, or he had a serious drinking problem. You can often spot an alcoholic from the dilated blood vessels on their face.

"Um, no, Sir. No I wouldn't."

"Hmmm. Good. Thank you, Miss Cassidy. I will see you at dinner tonight."

I was certainly curious about the reason for that question, but wasn't about to ask. I took my leave of Nathaniel and made my way to Cassandra's room. I found her in the same spot she had been the day before, although she looked in better spirits this time. Wesley was awake. Cassandra had her hands wrapped underneath his arms, holding him upright in her lap as he sucked at his fingers and scanned her face with intent eyes. Beaming, she rubbed her nose against his. "Have a seat," she instructed me, eyes still glued to her son. "Tell me, Miss Cassidy, do you have any children of your own?"

My throat constricted. I hadn't thought about the baby in days. "No. I don't. And please, call me Anna."

"Have you ever been in love, Anna?"

"Yes. Yes, I think I was." A nervous giggle slipped from me unbidden. Without even meaning to, Cassandra went straight for the heart, didn't she? "I mean, what is love, anyway?" I countered. "You know researchers who have looked at love throughout the ages have come up with a whole bunch of different categories? *Eros* is plain old sexual desire and passion. Then there's the kind of love we have for family, friends. Things we value. *Agape* is love that is truly selfless, placing someone above your own needs and wants without even having to think twice about it. There's obsessive love. And then *pragma* is what some call what develops over time between two people in a committed relationship, with sustained active goodwill and understanding." I realized I was rambling. The topic had me feeling on edge for some reason I didn't fully understand. But Cassandra was listening attentively. She watched me, biting her lower lip as I wrapped up my little monologue. "But how long can you keep that up? Before the goodwill and understanding just wear out?" I stopped, suddenly embarrassed.

Cassandra was thoughtful. "On the other hand, biology shows us how our bodies experience it. Lust causes our glands to release testosterone and estrogen. But when we're falling in love, our bodies flood with dopamine, serotonin, vasopressin..."

I sat back and studied the woman across from me. Before that moment I don't think it had occurred to me to see Cassandra as an individual, as someone with actual thoughts, interests, and ideas of her own. She wasn't just a victim of fateful circumstance. She was a real person. She was intelligent, and surely she was experiencing her plight just as keenly as I was my own.

The baby gurgled, drawing our attention. I was struck with a thought. "So if you people-I mean, the Sentient-live so much longer than the rest of us, does that mean Wesley is going to be a baby for a longer time?"

Cassandra shook her head, a lock of red hair falling in front of her face. "I don't claim to understand the exact physiology of it all. That's more the specialty of the Valois family. But I can tell you that the rate we age slows down over time. In the beginning we're pretty much the same as you. Take my niece and nephew, for instance. How old would you guess they were, by human standards?"

I considered. "I guess I would put Julian at about ten, and Evelyn maybe fifteen or so."

"Julian really is only thirteen, so you aren't too far off there. But Evelyn is, let's see...twenty-four years old now. But then of course, Wesley is half human, so I really couldn't say."

"Huh." I was curious to know what age that put Cassandra and her brothers at, but I wasn't sure if the same rule about never asking a lady's age also applied to preternatural ladies. Instead I said, "You said another family 'specialized' in Sentient physiology. So does that mean each family has a particular area of expertise?"

"Things just sort of naturally evolved that way. You know alchemy was the precursor to early chemistry, right? But there are plenty of different areas to study. Not every member of a family shares the same interests, but in general each has a focus. Here we work with spagyrics." She must have seen the blank look on my face. "Plant alchemy. We study plants and how to extract the components needed to create the desired tinctures. That's how my family does our part to contribute to the cause. We Sentient are expected to continually strive to learn about the way things work. Only by truly understanding the world can we develop the power to control it." Her tone had turned scornful and she reminded me very much of Jameson at that moment.

I would have loved for Cassandra to have kept talking about the Sentient, to hear more about this enigmatic group with claims to mysterious powers whose affairs I had managed to get swept up in. But just then she let a yawn escape and the baby began to whine. I reminded myself that, no matter what else she was, this woman was still a new mother who probably wasn't getting a lot of sleep. Even locked in her room as she was, seeing to the needs of a newborn would certainly have been keeping her busy. "Thank you for explaining. I'll leave you two be now," I told her.

"Before you go," Cassandra began, then wavered. "That is, how is my father?"

"Well, he definitely doesn't seem to be feeling well. Figuring out why is no easy task, seeing as his being sick is apparently impossible in the first place." I shook my head. "I don't know why I'm here. I mean, I know the reasons I've been given, but no matter what I come up with, I doubt your brother will believe me."

"Maybe not my brother. But my father will hear you out. If you can at least make him more comfortable..."

"Of course. I'll do what I can for him," I said. I looked around her room, at all of the trappings. Cassandra reminded me of a princess locked in a tower. Too bad her hair wasn't several yards longer. "They let me have a copy of the key to your room. I've been told in no uncertain terms that I am not allowed to leave here, and if I try, I will allegedly regret it. Tell me, what is it that stops you from just walking out of this place?"

"Some things are stronger than wood and steel." Cassandra let out a heavy sigh, laden with emotions I could only imagine. "Locking us in here is probably more a measure for keeping certain people out. Although it's a bit late to be worrying about that." Her lips formed a tight smile, one without any humor, and her eyes flashed. In light of her answer I only had more questions than ever, but that was apparently all Cassandra was willing to volunteer at the time.

"Would it be alright if I visit again tomorrow?" I asked.

Her smile softened and she glanced up at me. I remembered the first time I set eyes on her, how her beauty had seemed so out of place in the ordinary surroundings of my workplace. "I would like that," she said.

I found myself with a lot of time on my hands during the hours that stretched between seeing Nathaniel and Cassandra in the mornings and when I was expected at dinner. Other meals were informal. Usually Deborah would lay out a spread downstairs, and by the time I got there Victor and his family had already come and gone. Nathaniel and Cassandra were the only two who had their food delivered at those times, due to their respective situations. Otherwise I mostly I passed the time in my room, reading books taken from the library with Dinah curled up beside me. I also took up exploring the gardens nearly every day.

There was one time I returned to my room after my stroll and found that I had visitors, despite the fact that I could have sworn I had locked my door before leaving. Julian sat on my bed playing with Dinah. For the first time, I caught sight of his face when it wasn't kept guarded. He had a look of unrestrained pleasure as he ran his hand beneath the blankets, the cat pouncing after it. Meanwhile, Evelyn stood by the armoire appraising my clothes. She merely glanced at me when I entered and then went back to browsing, drawing out the items that caught her interest for a closer look.

I wasn't sure how to react. "Um, hi?"

"What's his name?" Julian asked in response.

"My cat? Dinah."

The boy scrunched up his face. "What kind of name is that?"

"She's a girl. It's a girl name."

Julian withdrew his hand from under the blankets and pet the cat. With his other hand he pointed to where I had hung my stethoscope around the bed knob. "What's that?" He had seemingly gotten over his unwillingness to speak to me any more than was necessary.

"It's called a stethoscope. That's what nurses and doctors use to listen to their patients' hearts and lungs. Do you want to try it out on Dinah?"

The boy's blue eyes widened, but with delight rather than the alarm I usually saw reflected there. He nodded his head.

I helped Julian position the stethoscope so that he could listen to the cat's heartbeat. "I hear it!" he exclaimed. After a minute of listening he slipped the buds out of his ears. "Maybe I'll be a nurse or doctor someday, and I can have one of these too."

"Don't be stupid," Evelyn interjected from where she was still making herself at home with my things on the other side of the room. "Nurses and doctors are for humans. And who cares about them?"

Julian glowered at his sister. "Grandfather needs a nurse."

Evelyn threw a sneering look in my direction, her curtain of black hair spilling over her shoulder as she turned. "He doesn't need her. She can't help him. Grandfather is dying of a broken heart."

"He's *not* dying!" Julian denied, sliding from the bed. Dinah leapt down at the sound of his raised voice, tail held stiffly in the air.

"Don't be such a child," the girl muttered, holding one of my favorite shirts up in front of herself.

Suddenly both children swung around to face the door, as if in response to some signal I couldn't detect. I looked over my shoulder, but saw nothing, heard nothing. Chalk another one up to superhuman Sentient senses. I turned again to see Evelyn putting my shirt on its hanger in the armoire, and Julian lifting the stethoscope from his shoulders. He handed it to me. "I like your cat," he told me as they both made for the door. And then they were gone.

At dinner that evening no one spoke much. I think we were all focused on pretending we didn't notice Nathaniel breathing heavily as he pushed his food around his plate and occasionally lifted a forkful to his mouth. When the time came, he once again tried to excuse himself from accompanying us to the sitting room.

"Oh, come, Father!" Victor persuaded, dropping a hand on Nathaniel's shoulder. "You are the very heart of this tradition! We get to see you so seldom these days. The children especially look forward to this time with you, always asking if you will be joining us."

Nathaniel puffed his cheeks and exhaled loudly, but waved toward the doorway and said, "Go on, then. I will make my way there in my own good time."

I waited until all of the others had left the dining room before approaching Nathaniel's seat at the head of the table. "If I may be blunt, you're in pretty bad shape. I realize you probably don't want your family to see just how bad, but if I'm here as your nurse, I'm going to have to insist you at least let me help you to the other room. I'll just walk with you, in case you need me." Nathaniel's face fell, but he nodded. I waited while he pushed himself up to standing. I linked my arm through his and we started heading for the dining room door. I took slow, measured steps to match his shuffling ones.

Out in the hall, Nathaniel patted my hand. "You have a kind soul, my dear," he murmured. "Your family must be quite proud of you." I felt a tightness in my chest, but didn't reply. He didn't need to know about the heart attack that killed my father when I was in high school, or the strained relationship I had with my mother that left us barely talking to one another except for the occasional phone call to check in and make sure the other was still alive. He could interpret my silence however he wished.

When finally we neared the entrance to the drawing room, I released Nathaniel's arm just before we reached the threshold. He motioned for me to enter ahead of him. I strode over to the sofa and sat, resolving to keep my temper in check, even if goaded as I had been the night before.

Victor poured the drinks as usual. As he passed them around, Evelyn held on to one for her grandfather while he lowered himself into his chair. His color wasn't good, his face ashen. I watched the rise and fall of his chest and didn't even have to count to know that his breathing was too fast. "Here you are, Grandfather," Evelyn said as she handed him his glass.

The rest of us sipped our drinks while Nathaniel caught his breath. Once he had composed himself, he tipped his glass back and took a mouthful of his own liquor. "Zahira, tell me," he croaked after swallowing harshly, "how are the children doing in their studies?" I experienced a pang of pity that he felt obligated to partake and make small talk, even when it was so clear he felt awful.

Zahira looked to her children. "Oh, they do well enough. Evelyn especially has shown great talent. She is, perhaps, a little too clever for her own good. Of course, then there are the times when neither of them is to be found when I call them for lessons."

"Ah, we only get to be children but once," Nathaniel said, his voice brimming with amusement despite being weak.

"Until one cousin or another discovers how to reverse the aging process entirely, that is," Jameson joked. At least I assumed it was a joke. There was a hint of the devil in the smile he aimed at me from where he leaned against the wall. I found myself smiling back. When I looked away I caught Victor watching us, a fire blazing in his eyes. The look made me shiver, which is perhaps ironic, but at the same time I took a sort of vindictive pleasure in getting his whiskers in a twist.

It was after only another sip or two that Nathaniel deemed his familial duty met and made to leave. "I apologize for not staying longer, but I do hear my bed calling."

"Mind if I accompany you upstairs?" I asked, setting my glass down on an end table.

"Not at all." I resumed my place by his side. We said goodnight to the others. Five sets of eyes followed our slow progress out of the room. After a faltering ascent up the grand staircase, I escorted Nathaniel to his chambers before telling him I would be right back after grabbing my equipment from my room.

When I returned, Nathaniel was waiting for me in his sitting room.

"Have a seat," I instructed. He collapsed onto the divan with a sigh. I moved my stethoscope around his chest and listened. There was no denying the crackling noise I heard was fluid built up in his lungs. I told him as much.

"Nathaniel, let's cut to the chase. I don't understand what I'm doing here. If I had to guess, I would say you're suffering from heart failure. In normal circumstances you could be treated with medications, which I don't have. But that doesn't matter, because I've been told you can't possibly be sick in the first place anyway. So what exactly is it you expect from me?"

Nathaniel looked past me, eyes glazed over, as he replied. "Heart failure. From what you have been able to gather, is there any indication as to what the cause might be?"

"Nothing that I can tell, no. Diuretics could help treat your symptoms, but without a diagnosis we wouldn't know what the cure might be. Is there no way you would go see a doctor?"

Nathaniel grunted. "In my case I wonder if the cause is something your doctors will have never seen before. Either way, any lab work they did on me would surely alert them to my unique physiology. I'm sure our own people could concoct something akin to your drugs, we just haven't needed to in such a long time. And I really would rather not draw any unnecessary attention to my family at this time, given the circumstances..." His voice trailed off. Several seconds passed before he seemed to gather himself again. "There were some who would object to Cassandra delivering at your birth center. But she assured me that it was a less interventional setting than the hospital, and that there should be no need to do blood work or anything of that sort. And even if they decided they wanted to, she could refuse. It is customary for other female members of a household to help the woman deliver her baby at home, but here there is only Zahira and, well...given the sensitive nature of this particular pregnancy and child, I ended up giving Cassandra my blessing to go to the birth center."

"Could one of you here at Willow Glen make up some sort of treatment, like a diuretic?" I pressed.

"Mm," was the only answer he gave, his eyes continuing to stare straight ahead. I looked over to see that he was gazing toward the portrait of his wife.

"You know, Miss Cassidy, sometimes I wonder if I haven't brought this upon myself. If maybe this isn't what I've actually been wanting."

"What, you mean to join your wife?"

I felt a draft then and realized the sliding glass doors to the balcony had been left open, leaving only the screen in place. The air wafting in was balmy, but I felt the hairs on my arms stand on end.

When I looked back down I saw that Nathaniel had his eyes fixed on me once more. "You do realize you present quite a problem, my dear? Only humans in our employ are permitted to know the truth about the Sentient, and then they are considered in our service for life. My daughter made a regrettable mistake when she involved you in our business. And I daresay Victor thinks he has the solution." I was taken by surprise when I felt Nathaniel take my hand in his own. I glanced down. His skin felt dry, papery. "As long as I am able to make the argument that you are serving a purpose here, making yourself useful, I can hold him at bay. I am still the head of this family. But my eldest has ever tried to overreach himself."

My throat welled with a mix of emotions, not the least of which were the fear and anger I had grown so familiar with. I tried to swallow them back down. "Well. I can certainly try to help make you more comfortable. I suggest you stack your pillows and sleep as upright as you can. It should make breathing a little easier at night."

"That is a wonderful prospect."

"Limit your salt intake. Drink water, but not too much. Try some deep breathing exercises to keep your lungs open and clear. And don't overexert yourself."

"Thank you Miss Cassidy. I will see you in the morning, then."

"Good night, Nathaniel."

I slipped my hand from his and returned to my own room, weighed down with a sense of helplessness and dread that had only intensified since the moment I had arrived at Willow Glen Manor.

6

July 28th, 2013

Someone rang the doorbell today. The sound of the chimes reverberated throughout the still house, the furniture itself seemed to hum with it. I was overcome with the absurd urge to hide. Instead I stood frozen, all but holding my breath as I waited for whoever it was to go away. I'm not sure how much time passed like that, but eventually I realized the crisis was over and I could relax my aching muscles.

Then I thought, *How could I be so stupid?!* What if the person at the door had been...had been someone who...someone like...

I wasn't even able to put my thoughts into words.

I've decided I need to get myself out of this house and venture into the real world, just for a little while. Soon.

I made my usual rounds the next day. Checking in on Nathaniel yielded nothing encouraging. He was making less urine and gaining weight as time went on. His body was clearly retaining fluid, sending his already-stressed heart into overdrive. He was in a despondent mood that morning. I offered some more tips for keeping comfortable, then my worries and I left him alone with his.

As I was making my way to Cassandra's bower, as she called it, I came across Frederick running a cloth over the gilded frames of two paintings displayed in the hallway. The casings gleamed from his attentions, but for the first time I was aware that the butler appeared rather harried. With so few servants in such a large home, even with only some of the rooms in use they must have been hard pressed to keep up with the maintenance, sharing their duties. Frederick tilted his head at me in acknowledgment, but soon had finished his polishing and took off.

I paused to view the paintings. I had passed by them many times but had never really taken the time to study them. The one on the right showed a bearded man in robes extending a hand toward a peculiar apparatus where it sat perched on a shelf. The device looked like two flasks, one sitting higher than the other, connected by a tube and filled with some sort of shimmering fluid. Reading through the book on the history of alchemy since then would teach me that this is called an alembic.

The second painting was suspended a few feet to the left of the first. On its canvas another man held a beaker aloft in one hand and pointed to it with the other. In fact, both men appeared to be pointing. It almost looked as if they were gesturing toward each other.

Or to some place in between.

I moved closer and that's when I found the marking of a hidden entrance, the purification symbol scored into the wall between where the paintings hung.

That was how I found the location of the other secret room I came to know about at Willow Glen Manor. My pulse quickened at the discovery, but at the time there was no way for me to gain access to the room that lay beyond. I smoothed the palm of my hand over the ridges of the carving. "Damn."

Admitting defeat, I continued on my way, mind simmering with this new knowledge.

I unlocked the doors to Cassandra's room and knocked gently as I let myself in. "Good morning. Mind if I-oh!" I was taken aback to see that I was not the only visitor there. Cassandra and Jameson both turned toward me as I entered, smiling about whatever it was they had been discussing. Cassandra had her legs tucked up on the sofa in her usual spot, Wesley cradled in her arms. Jameson lounged in the chair I usually took for myself, long legs stretched in front of him and crossed at the ankles.

"Should I come back some other time?" I asked.

Cassandra patted the couch cushion beside her. "No, no, please come sit," she trilled. I crossed the room and sat in the spot she had indicated, crossing my legs and folding my hands over my knees. I held my back straight, acutely aware of the company. Why was I suddenly nervous again? It's not as if Jameson was...well, Victor.

"We were just reminiscing about some of our favorite childhood exploits," Jameson explained.

I raised my brow. "I can't even picture the two of you as children."

"Well, it has been quite some time," he replied.

"Can I assume you were the chief troublemaker in those days?"

"I'll have you know that Cassandra was no saint herself," he disputed as he rubbed a hand around the crown of his head, mussing his coppery hair before smoothing it back into place. "She was never one to mind the rules. She was usually just too clever to get caught, but when she did, her punishment was always outrageously less severe than mine and Victor's. One of the many perks of being Father's favorite."

"A trend that has apparently followed us into adulthood," Cassandra added in a flat voice. She hunched down over the baby and cooed, "But if I had followed the rules, I would never have met *you*," before kissing him on the top of his head.

"Heaven forbid it had been Victor or I who knocked boots with a human and wound up pregnant. It would have been off with our heads for sure," Jameson teased, but the atmosphere in the room had shifted and no one laughed. I watched a troubled crease form on his forehead as he stared at the floor.

A silence stretched out before us, finally broken when Wesley sneezed three times in quick succession, delighting his mother. "Even your sneezes are adorable!" she exclaimed.

Jameson's face curved into a half-hearted smile, but through his eyes I could see that his mind was still somewhere far away. Somewhere distressing. I wanted to draw him back. It was with some surprise I recognized that I wanted to bring his attention back my way, along with the tingling warmth it brought with it. I managed to shock myself with that realization. I shook my head, trying to dislodge whatever absurd notions had come over me.

"So, um, Julian seems like a good kid," was the first thing I thought to say.

Jameson's eyes focused on my face, making me feel equal parts giddy and ridiculous. "Only because he hasn't been around long enough to be corrupted by his parents yet," he responded. "Give him time. Eventually he will be just as much of a pretentious brat as his sister."

"*Jameson!*" Cassandra scolded before dissolving into a fit of laughter.

Seeing the two of them together, it was clear that they got along better than anyone else in the house. It was evident that both respected their father, even when they didn't agree with him. Otherwise, the members of the Dorn family seemed at times to barely tolerate one another. That was not the case with Jameson and Cassandra. They adored one another.

"Well I, for one, am dying to hear about some of these childhood escapades. Come on, out with it," I coaxed.

Jameson and Cassandra looked at one another, both grinning.

"Hmm," Jameson considered for a minute. "There was that time you turned Ms. Fairchild's hair bright green."

"She deserved it! That woman was the most exacting, merciless dictator to ever darken our doorway!"

Jameson tilted his head toward me. "She was our governess. Briefly," he said by way of explanation.

I wasn't sure I liked the sound of that. "Wait a second, I thought humans were in your service for life?"

"When it became clear that Ms. Fairchild and we children weren't quite...compatible, she was transferred to another Sentient family. One with more biddable children, presumably."

"Ah." I rested my chin in my hand, waiting to hear more.

"Even at a young age, Cassandra was skilled with the spagyrics. She cooked up some sort of tonic. I distracted Ms. Fairchild with some idiotic antics, I can't remember exactly what now. While I drew the governess' ire, Cassandra tipped some of her sinister brew into the woman's tea. After a slap on the hand, I was ordered to take a seat and not get up until instructed to do so."

"Where was Victor during all of this?" I wanted to know.

It was Cassandra who answered. "Off somewhere being a prig. Any time we let him in on any of our schemes, he usually tattled before we had a chance to pull them off. We'd be in hot water, but he would usually get reprimanded, too, for being a snitch."

Jameson continued the story. "I watched from my chair, nursing stinging knuckles, as Ms. Fairchild returned to her tea. She went on muttering to herself, and it seemed like we waited an eternity before she finally took a sip. Almost instantly the change began. Bright green, like the color of a parrot's feathers, seeped into her hair from the scalp outward. It advanced until there wasn't a single gray strand left. When we couldn't stop roaring with laughter, she caught on and held up her spoon to look at her reflection. We had heard her yell plenty of times before, but never knew she could scream like that."

"It sounds like you have quite the talent," I said to Cassandra.

"Well, to be perfectly honest, I had been going for purple hair. Still not quite sure where I went wrong." We all laughed for a long while at that, and it occurred to me that I couldn't remember the last time I had laughed like that. It felt good.

"Only now that I'm an adult can I see that the old witch just really, really needed to get laid," Cassandra said.

"To hear such talk from my little sister!" Jameson accused in mock indignation.

"Yes, well, I've learned from the best," Cassandra replied, swinging her fist into her brother's arm.

Time passed quickly as Cassandra and Jameson went on musing over the many pranks they had played on others over the years. It seemed no member of the household had been safe.

While the three of us chuckled, Wesley let loose a whimper that soon grew into a wail of hungry displeasure. "Time to feed the baby," Cassandra announced.

"Aaand, that's my cue," Jameson said, springing from his chair.

"I'll give you some privacy," I said.

"See you tomorrow!" Cassandra called out as she began loosening the buttons of her shirt.

Jameson and I walked side by side out in the hall. "Tell me another secret," I implored.

"A secret? About this place? About one of us? Hmm, let's see." He stroked his chin thoughtfully. "Oh, here's one! I'm *famished*!"

I scrunched my eyebrows together at him.

"What? You didn't know I was hungry, did you? And now you do. Come, let's go pester Deborah." He extended an arm, indicating that I should walk in front. The corridor was perfectly wide enough for two people to walk side by side. I stepped ahead anyway, all too aware of the view he was getting, and wondered if that was why he had wanted me to go in front of him. That thought made me self-conscious, but I can't lie, there might have been an extra sway in my hips.

In the kitchen, Deborah was pulling fresh brown loaves of bread out through the arched opening of one of the room's two brick ovens. My mouth began to water as soon as the aroma rolled over us. I realized that I had missed out on breakfast during my time with Nathaniel and then in the bower, but lunch was still a ways off. I was famished, too.

"Deborah, my one true love!" Jameson exclaimed, hoisting himself up to sit on the dark quartz countertop.

The housekeeper scowled but her eyes glinted with amusement. "You!" Tugging the oven mitts from her hands, she grabbed a dish towel and snapped it at Jameson's dangling legs. "How many times do I have to tell you to leave me be when I'm at my work?"

Jameson shook his head solemnly. "I know. I've tried so hard to respect your wishes, but I simply cannot bear to be too long away from your tantalizing beauty."

Deborah snorted as she set to slicing vegetables for a salad at the cutting board. "Tantalizing beauty, my rump," she retorted, cheeks turning rosy.

"Yes, I have to agree that *is* one part of a woman I find most alluring." Jameson winked at me, and to my chagrin I felt my own face begin to burn. Deborah clapped a hand to her mouth to stifle a giggle.

Jameson reached for where the bread sat cooling, but his hand was slapped away. "You'll burn your fingers! Now if you're here because you can't wait for lunch to be set out, then I suppose if you take yourselves to one of the tables out back, I could bring you a little something to nibble on."

"That would be splendid! Only..."

"What is it now?"

"You know how I do love your bruschetta with the brie melted on top."

"Your wish is my command, Your Highness. Just get out of my hair and I'll bring you whatever your dark heart desires."

Jameson clutched his hands to his chest. "My dark heart that bleeds from want of your love!" Deborah made to swat at him again, but before her hand made contact he had slid down from the counter and side-stepped away. He waved for me to follow him through the door that led outside.

We stepped out onto the stone terrace that ran along the back of the house. It held tables and chairs for dining or relaxing outdoors. It was there we waited until Deborah stepped out with a plateful of the snack Jameson had requested. We thanked her and began to eat while she returned to her work.

"So, you folks still rely on consuming food to fuel your bodies, huh?" I commented. "That seems awfully mundane."

Jameson looked about to deliver a comeback when we heard voices nearby. Craning around, I saw Victor and Evelyn ambling up the garden path together. It didn't seem they had noticed our presence yet.

"...the audacity to allow it to live, shaming the entire family in this way."

"Like you said, Father, it will be a magnificent day for all Sentient everywhere when you assume your place at the head of-" Victor had spotted us and extended an arm in front of his daughter, bringing her up short. Evelyn looked at him in surprise, then turned and saw what had stopped him.

"Fine day, isn't it?" Victor asked as he recovered himself and skipped up the terrace steps, his daughter following right behind.

"A fine day," Jameson said. There was a chill in his voice that hadn't been there moments before. "Perhaps not a magnificent day, but a fine one in any case."

Without any further attempt at conversation, Victor and Evelyn continued into the house, leaving an uneasy pall in their wake. Jameson stared at the door they had disappeared through. I saw that the hand he held on the tabletop was clenched into a fist. When he addressed me again it was with flat eyes that had shut me out. "I believe I've had enough," he told me, gesturing to the remaining food on the plate. "Please, stay and enjoy them. I'll see you tonight."

❖

I nodded and watched him disappear into the house. My innards felt as though they had shriveled at the very sight of Victor and his daughter, and my own appetite had spoiled. As much as I shuddered at the thought of any sort of contact with that man, there was something I thought I should talk to him about, and so I returned the half-full plate to the housekeeper and went in search of him.

I found Victor and Evelyn in the drawing room. The father sat forward in the chair at the writing desk, expounding on some topic or other to his daughter, hands waving in the air before him. Evelyn stood in front of him and hung on his every word. Victor fell silent when I entered the room, and both turned frosty gazes my way.

I cleared my throat. "Sorry to interrupt. I'm sure whatever you were talking about was of the utmost, earth-shattering importance, as with everything you have to say." Provoking those two was not the wisest course of action, but I had a hard time holding in my revulsion. Evelyn's upper lip curled in a snarl. I rushed to explain myself before she had a chance to strike back. "But I think you might want to hear this."

Victor crossed his arms in front of his chest and leaned back in his chair, managing to look down his nose at me despite the fact that I was standing and he was sitting. "By all means, then, don't keep us waiting."

"Fine. I know you don't think your father can suffer from heart failure, and with the tools I have here I can't tell you for sure what the cause of his problem is. What I *can* tell you is that the symptoms are like those of heart failure. If we can't be sure how to cure him, we can at least try to relieve the symptoms. You guys are the ones with the superhuman talent with plants and compounds. Could you try to concoct something like a diuretic? Something to get rid of all the extra fluid his heart is struggling to pump?"

"You would do well to watch your tone," Evelyn warned me. She certainly didn't sound like any teenage girl I had ever known. I met her cold stare, then averted my eyes. As riled as I was, I knew the sensible thing to do was stop before pushing these people too far.

"I asked Nathaniel about one of you trying to draw up something like that for him, but he seemed hesitant. I think he's become depressed with everything that's going on. Maybe one of you could reason with him." When I looked back to Victor, his eyes had taken a break from staring me down and were trained on the carpet. His jaw worked back and forth. After considering for a minute, he looked up again.

"We could probably figure out how to mix up something like your diuretics. No Sentient has needed such treatments in so long that we've fallen out of practice with medicine. Cassandra had the most skill with the plants." He spat rather than spoke his sister's name, and I noticed his use of the past tense. He turned to his daughter, his eyes softening. "But Evelyn is a fair hand, too. This girl soaks up knowledge like a sponge. If we research the components of those drugs together, Kitten, do you think you might try to make something like that for your grandfather?"

Evelyn gave a pert nod, her face attaining a softer, rosier look at her father's attention and words of praise. "I can do it," she said, no hint of doubt in her words.

"Good." Victor unfolded himself from the chair and stood. "Now run along for the time being. I need to have some words with our guest, here."

There was laughter in the curves of her face as Evelyn walked by me and left me alone with her father. Victor ambled closer to me and drew to a stop only a couple of feet away. "It seems you need a reminder that you are here by the grace of our good will, Miss Cassidy, temporary as it may be. At any moment I could change my mind and do with you what I've thought was necessary all along. My father and brother will grumble a bit at me going against their wishes, but in time they will move on and forget, as with any minor inconvenience. For that is all you are."

I could feel the stifling rot of his words blow over me with his breath. In the face of such a direct insult, I forgot all about being sensible. I angled my head up to look him in the eyes. "You talk awfully big, Victor Dorn. Compensating for something, are you?"

I saw the fury flare behind his eyes and had a fleeting moment to regret my words and feel frightened. Victor dropped a hand on my shoulder and steered me toward another part of the room. I wondered what he was doing, but didn't dare question him just then. He led me to the set of shelves against the wall, where there were figurines and other various objects on display. "There is something I think you fail to understand about us, Miss Cassidy, and your situation here. Do you see these urns here on this shelf?"

His hand exerted a gentle but insistent pressure on the back of my neck, forcing me forward for a closer look. One of the shelves held little vase-like vessels in a row. One was a shallow dish made of some kind of white stone with flecks of gray, another was tall and slender and looked to be made from obsidian. "I see them," I bit out, the skin at the back of my neck prickling where he touched it.

Victor reached his other hand out and, with a single finger, traced a pattern on the wood of the shelf in front of the urns. It was the shape of a triangle, easy for me to follow with my eyes. With that simple motion, jets of flame leapt suddenly from the mouths of each vessel, much too close to my face. Rising several inches into the air, the licking flames were powerful enough that they roared as they flared, a veritable inferno along the length of the shelf. Bending over the oven to take out dinner was nothing compared to the heat of this enchanted fire. I tried to jerk away, but Victor's grip held me in place. The flames died down almost as quickly as they had begun, but not before I caught the scent of singed hair. I reached my hands up to pat at my forehead, my eyebrows and lashes. I wasn't on fire, but the skin of my face was warm to the touch. The urns looked just as they had before that little trick of Victor's, without a trace of charring. A cold sweat sprung up along my hairline, a strange sensation against the heat of my face.

Victor released his hold on me and took a step back. I spun around to face him, my heart pounding.

"You know what they say about playing with fire," Victor told me, sounding well pleased with himself. His eyes narrowed on mine, his voice dropped. Disgust replaced smugness. "Just give me an excuse. Trust me, I would love nothing more." He backed away one slow step at a time, then turned and left the room.

When I was alone I covered my face with my hands. I remained like that until the beating of my heart had wound back down to a normal rhythm. "Jesus," I whispered into my hands. "He must have a hell of a lot to compensate for."

I tore my hands from my face and glanced anxiously around the room, making sure no one had snuck up on me and heard those words. There was no one, and I promised myself I would try to be more careful about what I said from then on. Subdued for the time being, I slinked away to my bedroom.

Scanning the pages of the *History of Alchemy* book confirms that the alchemical symbol for fire is, of course, a right-side up triangle.

Other than the extra nerves lodged in my chest from my encounter with Victor earlier, dinner that night was little changed from previous evenings. Strained dialogue, the sound of Nathaniel hacking instead of eating. I half-expected Victor to gloat, but it seemed he had chosen instead to pretend I didn't exist.

In the drawing room afterwards, Nathaniel missed the first time he reached out to take his glass of brandy from Evelyn, his hand swiping through empty air.

"Is something the matter, Nathaniel?" Zahira asked from where she perched at the edge of her own seat.

"Bah, just clumsy is all," her father-in-law answered. He snatched the glass and tossed it back.

Victor clapped a hand on his father's shoulder. "There you go! That's how a man fortifies himself," he declared.

"Oh?" Jameson said. "What man told you that?"

"It just so happens, little brother," Victor stated, "that I am in too good of a mood to let even your irritating prattle bring me down."

"That's a pity."

"Enough!" Nathaniel barked, his voice raspy. "I'm sure Miss Cassidy does not want to listen to the two of you bickering every day and every night."

"Don't worry, Father," Jameson reassured him. "Victor and I generally keep as far away from each other as possible during the day."

Nathaniel grunted. At first I thought he was angry, but then saw him double over clinging to his stomach. "Nathaniel?" The others turned to look at him when I called his name. He said nothing for a moment, but remained unmoving with his hands locked over his abdomen. Jameson took a step toward his father.

Finally Nathaniel spoke up in a small voice. "I think perhaps I need to retire already. I apologize for the disruption. Please, everybody stay here and continue without me." I was ready to help him in any case, springing from my seat. Nathaniel threw up a hand. "Please, Miss Cassidy. I really must insist this time. Just a little stomach upset, I'm afraid."

Fighting the urge to tell him where to stick his stomach upset and walk him to his room anyway, I faltered before dropping back down on the sofa. All of us in the sitting room watched his shambling progress as he made his exit. I couldn't help but sneak an anxious look at the urns on the shelf. A pang of nausea jolted through me at the reminder of Victor's hold over me.

When the dragging footsteps from the hall could no longer be heard, Victor tipped back his glass and then wagged his head from side to side. "To think that wretched individual hobbling away to hide himself in his room used to be one of the most revered men among the Sentient."

"He still is," Jameson countered icily.

"Not for long. Just wait until the others see him in his current condition. They will fear its implications, yes, but they will lose all regard for our esteemed sire. Who can respect one such as that?" He turned a probing gaze onto me. "Have you made any progress as far as discovering the source of his decline yet?"

He knew very well what my answer would be. Knowing that my life could depend on proving my usefulness in curing the unknowable was not very encouraging. I crossed and then uncrossed my legs, grappling for a response that would satisfy. Unfortunately, I don't think such a thing existed. "I can tell you what his symptoms suggest. I can tell you what it would mean for a human, for a patient in a healthcare setting. For your father, I don't know what it means. I can help ease some of the symptoms, but no, I don't know what could be making a person such as him sick."

Victor seemed to glow with triumph; he really was on some kind of high that night. "I see. So if you can offer no insight on what is making him sick in the first place so that we can stop it, perhaps my dear little brother can explain to us why, exactly, your presence here is still required."

Jameson clenched his jaw. "Drop it, Victor."

Victor's countenance suddenly turned ugly. "You may be used to getting your way, but I will be damned if I let history repeat itself. Just keep in mind this family is in enough disgrace as it is without you pulling any of your stunts. Zahira, children. Come."

Without a word, Victor's family lined up and followed him out the door, only Evelyn looking back to aim a withering glare our way.

I could feel Jameson smoldering from where he stood a few feet from me. Any good humor I had caught from him earlier that day had been thoroughly leached away. Saying nothing, he pivoted and marched over to the liquor cabinet, where he pulled down another bottle of booze and refilled his glass. I watched him for a while. He gave no indication of even being aware I was still in the room. I was disappointed, but also annoyed. Refusing to stay only to be ignored, I slipped away without a word.

Dinah, at least, acknowledged my presence when I stepped into my bedroom, meowing and stretching her forepaws out in front of her. She hopped down from the bed and crossed to her food dish.

After mumbling a greeting, I began to strip off my clothes. Through the window it looked on the verge of rain. Swollen clouds hovered in the darkening sky. An electric tension hung in the air, matching the atmosphere inside of Willow Glen.

Sighing, I pulled a black tank top on over my head. Clad in only that and my underwear I lunged into the bed and luxuriated in the feel of the satiny sheets against my skin. The whirring of my mind took time to slow down, but eventually I drifted into sleep.

I woke with a start some time later. I lay still, holding my breath, trying to pinpoint what it was that had woken me. A muffled drone reached my ears, erratic in pitch and volume. With an earsplitting *crash*, my room lit up as bright as day. Recovering my wits from the depths of slumber, I recognized that the promised storm had arrived and the booming thunder and lightning were likely what had wrenched me from my sleep. As soon as I had the thought, the driving rain began. I noticed Dinah frozen on the other side of the bed, fur standing on end. "It's okay," I whispered to her, rubbing behind her ears. Another flash of lightning and roll of thunder sent her diving off the bed, raking her claws against the skin over my knuckles as she went.

"Ouch!" I sucked at the blood that had surfaced, a vitalizing coppery taste pricking my tongue. Despite the hour, I was wide awake once more.

Soon the thunder subsided and the rushing sound of the rain took over. It was then I understood there was still another noise I was hearing. The sound of voices.

Folding the covers back, I got out of bed and crept barefoot to the door of my room. I eased the door open warily and leaned out to listen.

It was definitely voices I was hearing. Voices raised in anger. Although I couldn't make out the words, I could discern the volleys being flung back and forth, first by one male voice and then by another. I felt my own heart rate pickup. Other people arguing had made me anxious as long as I could remember. My body reacted even when I wasn't involved in the dispute.

I squeezed my eyes shut and tried to convince myself that the argument I was hearing had nothing to do with me, and so I needn't worry about it. I was being a good little human, tucked away in my room and behaving myself. There was no reason for me to feel frightened. I was still persuading myself of this when I realized the yelling had stopped. There was the slamming of a door, and then nothing. *Thank God*, I thought as I opened my eyes.

A form was materializing out of the shadows down the corridor. Someone was approaching, fast. I squinted in the murk of the hallway. As the person drew nearer I saw that it was only Jameson and I put a hand to my chest, relieved.

But then I saw his face. I had never seen him looking so worked up about anything. His jaw was clenched, the lines of his face set in anger. And he was headed right for me.

"Jameson?" My voice sounded small and uncertain even to my own ears. He was only a few yards away, and closing. "Jameson, what are-"

He crashed into me, the weight of his body pressing me against the wall. When his lips collided with mine it was with enough force to knock the back of my head against the wood paneling. If it hurt, I didn't notice.

My initial shock didn't last long. Not when the heat of his mouth was so demanding, when the scratching of his stubble stung my face so sweetly, when the solid press of his arms snaked around my hips and his searing grip on the back of my thighs lifted me straight off the floor. With my legs wrapped around his waist, we stumbled back into my bedroom.

I don't think I need to say more except that what transpired then was pure, unadulterated *eros*. It was the passion my life had been lacking, and then some. It was exactly what I needed without even knowing I needed it.

Afterwards we lay catching out breath, sweat mingling down the length of our tangled bodies. I had to make a conscious effort not to laugh out loud in sheer exhilaration at how liberated I felt, with no rules to heed other than the pure physical responses of my body. I held back since something told me Jameson wasn't in the mood for laughter. But it was like my entire body was buzzing, and my mind, too.

We stayed that way for a few minutes, recovering, transforming back into our normal self-possessed selves. It was the blissful interlude when your body unwinds back into itself but your mind and senses are enlivened. I felt like I could stay just like that forever.

Jameson, apparently, could not. He soon rolled off of the bed, pulled his pants back on, and tugged his shirt over his head. And then he left without saying a word.

7

July 29th, 2013

I have to admit I wasn't looking forward to telling that part of my story. It's not my proudest moment. Then again, why should I feel guilty? It's not like I did anything wrong.

But still, I felt wretched the next day. Not so much about what had happened, but about the way it had happened. And the way it had ended.

I couldn't stop thinking about "what it meant." Why had Jameson done that? He had been enraged when he came barreling down the hallway. Sure the sex had been amazing (hadn't he told me once about their superior reflexes?), but I couldn't help but consider the idea that I had simply been a convenient target for his fury that had been instilled by someone else, an outlet for his pent-up aggression. If I was a different sort of person I would have just said, "Who cares?" Did it matter *why*? It happened. We both enjoyed it. End of story.

But that's not me, and in the end I just had no idea how to feel. I still don't, really. But I guess it doesn't matter anymore.

After the events of the previous night, the last thing I wanted to do was face Jameson in the light of day and confront what had happened. I planned to keep to my bedroom as much as possible.

When a rapping came at my door sometime around midmorning, my stomach was in my throat as I answered the door. It wasn't Jameson, but I can't say I was at all relieved to see that it was Evelyn instead. With no words of greeting, she held up a small crystal vial filled with a clear liquid. "My father thinks you will have a better chance of getting my grandfather to drink this," she said in a voice of iron.

"The diuretic, already?" I took the vial, both of us making sure not to touch the other in the process. I eyed its contents. "Okay. I'll see what I can do. And...thanks." I got the impression that Evelyn just barely stopped herself from rolling her eyes at me before walking away. There were some ways, at least, in which she did seem like your typical teenager. I didn't stay long, either, grabbing my medical equipment and making my way for Nathaniel's rooms right away.

Needless to say, there had been no improvement in his condition. His weight was up yet again, he felt lousy and was still disheartened. I did what I could to make him more comfortable, which was not much. Then I showed him the tonic Evelyn had made.

"What's this?" he asked,

"Your family made it for you. I asked them to. We hope it will work like the medication you would receive if you were a human being treated by a physician. It won't fix you, but it might make you feel better for a while."

Nathaniel said nothing for a long time. I started to think that he might not even answer. At last, with another of his great sighs, he pointed to the glass-topped table by his side. "Set it there. I suppose I ought to at least give it a try." I almost wished he would drink the stuff right in front of me, so I could be sure he took it. I had to allow the man some measure of pride, though. I let him be, and left his chambers to the sound of him mumbling something about the medicine probably tasting dreadful. Spirits were dragging as low as ever that day, but at least we had been offered a glimmer of hope. We would see how well the tincture did its job the next time I checked in on Nathaniel.

I started to make my way toward my own room when I caught sight of Julian in the hall up ahead. He had his ball with him, tucked under his arm. Before I could call out any greeting, I saw him reach up and hold his hand against the wall. Right in between the two paintings. Right where I had seen the symbol. I watched as part of the wall swung open at Julian's touch. The boy stepped back out of the door's path, and as he did so his ball slipped out from under his arm and bounced away through the opening and into the room beyond. Julian chased after it.

He left the door standing open behind him.

I held absolutely still for a moment, waiting to see if the boy would come back and shut the door. He didn't. I stole over to the entryway and stopped just outside. I glanced up and down the hallway to make sure there was no one to see me. Not seeing anybody, I poked my head around the threshold and peeked into the room. It looked like a conservatory of sorts. I could see no one from that vantage point. Breaking into a sweat at just the thought of what I was about to do, I held my breath and darted into the room.

Immediately I was immersed in air thick with humidity, permeated with the heady scent of earth and fertilizer. Rows of plants stretched down the length of the room. A long table ran along the wall on my left, strewn with various tools and equipment. I saw mortars and pestles of all different materials: marble, porcelain, granite, cast iron. I recognized the device from one of the portraits suspended just outside the entrance, the alembic. There were crucibles, and tubes and bottles of varying shapes and sizes. Shelves were installed above the table, lined with a multitude of small glass jars. I wasn't close enough to make out the handwritten names on their labels.

Julian was nowhere to be seen. The room resonated with the tinkling sound of flowing water and I began to take light, furtive steps toward the other side of the room to see if I could find where the noise was coming from.

As I made my way I glanced at the rows of plants. Many of them stood half as tall as me or taller. Some featured dense sprays of leaves, while others had limbs adorned with tiny buds or drooping with the weight of unfurled blossoms. Each had a placard with the plant's name and a date posted in front. I could read those at the end of the rows, nearest to me. I passed "Larkspur (*Delphinium*)", "Oleander *(Nerium oleander)*, and "Mexican Blue Palm *(Brahea armata)*", among others. Oddly, the dates with each ranged from the seventeen hundreds to the early twentieth century. I wasn't sure what they could signify; when each species had been identified? Shrugging to myself, I stepped to the next line of plants and saw something that made my heart leap into my throat.

There, at the other end of the row, was Evelyn. She appeared to be pruning one of the plants. She tugged a bough down in front of her, and was using the thumb and forefinger of one hand to pluck at it. She held the material she collected curled within the palm of her hand.

I realized I had frozen at the sight of her. She had only to turn her head in my direction and she would have been looking straight at me. If I didn't want her to see me I needed to get moving. Muscles tensed, I started to sneak away, moving in slow motion so that no sudden movement would draw Evelyn's eye.

Past the last row of plants I laid eyes on the source of the noise I had been hearing. There was a circular stone basin, its sides covered in markings and symbols I didn't recognize. I crept closer and peered inside. The basin was filled with water, but the mystifying part was that the water was swirling around and around without any obvious stimulus. I could see nothing that might be generating the whirlpool. Not waiting to puzzle over the phenomenon, I scurried behind the basin and ducked down to hide.

Thankfully it wasn't long before I heard the clapping of Evelyn's shoes against the floor and peered around the edge of the basin to see her making her way to the exit. I noticed her falter when she saw the door left gaping open. She shook her head, seeming irritated more than alarmed, and continued through and out of the room. I watched as the door swung shut behind her.

I waited a minute to make sure she was going to stay away before uncurling and stepping out from my hiding place. The sound of swilling water continued to fill the room, the heavy air continued to weigh down each breath I took. I looked all around, but still there was no sign of Julian. Curiosity overtook me, and I ventured toward the end of the room I hadn't gotten a look at yet, beyond the plants.

Up against the far wall there was a display cabinet of sorts. Drawing nearer, I could see the objects that decorated its shelves, which were many and varied. There was a necklace and other assorted bits of jewelry, little figurines, pieces of cut stone. Interesting though they might have been, I could see nothing special about the trinkets, and they seemed out of place in that room that otherwise seemed to serve mostly as a conservatory and laboratory. Peeling my eyes from them, I turned away.

Deciding I had better cut my explorations short before someone found me sticking my nose where they didn't think it belonged, I headed back for the room's exit. As I approached, I drew up short, my eyes scanning the door's surface. I searched that wooden expanse over and over, thinking I was just missing something. I wasn't. It dawned on me that there was no handle on the *inside* of the door, either. I sprung forward, closing the remaining distance between me and the door, and ran frantic hands over it. I felt around for any kind of latch or depression that my eyes might have missed. There was nothing. I let my hands fall to my side in defeat and, turning around, leaned back against the wall and slid down to the floor.

I tried not to panic and reviewed in my mind any possible courses of action I could take. I was coming up empty-handed. The only solution I could think of was that maybe Jameson would eventually notice my prolonged absence and come looking for me. But thinking of Jameson made my stomach twist in an even tighter knot than it already was. Perhaps it was best not to think at all for a while. I closed my eyes and did my best to clear my mind, to convince myself that things really weren't as bad as they seemed. I wasn't having much success. A scene kept replaying in my mind unbidden, one where I was stuck in the room for hours before Victor happened along and caught me there. Not thinking was not working.

Eventually I decided there was nothing for it but to continue exploring the room while I waited for inspiration to strike, or for someone to come save my sorry self. I pushed up off of the floor and approached the flowing waters of the basin again, wanting another look. The interior almost seemed to sparkle in the room's curious glow. I stretched out my arm, meaning to dip my fingers into the water.

"I don't think you should do that."

I cried out and spun around, clamping my hands over my mouth. There behind me stood Julian. I let out a sound that was half-cackle, half-sob. "You *scared* me!" I accused the boy, hissing through gritted teeth.

Julian looked terrified himself. His face was bled of all color and his lip actually trembled.

"Please," he said, "don't tell them I let you get in here. I didn't mean to, it was an accident."

The hammering in my chest began to subside as I realized where matters stood. Neither Julian nor I wanted anyone to know I had been in that hidden room. We would keep it a secret. I reached out and took the boy's small pale hand in my own. "I promise I won't tell, if you promise you won't." I saw comprehension spread over his face and some of his color returned. He gave a faint nod and even offered a slight smile. "Good," I said. "Now get us out of here!"

"Just a minute," the boy responded. "There's one more thing I wanted to do in here. I was just waiting for my sister to leave." His nose crinkled in distaste at the mention of Evelyn. "You can come watch, if you want," he told me before trotting away. I followed in his wake.

Julian drew up to the table covered with the collection of lab equipment. He stood before a large glass sphere with a spout shooting off at an upward angle from the side. Next to it on the table was a dish of dried leaves. I watched, intrigued, as Julian picked up a tool, a small scoop with a long handle. He pinched some of the herbs in his fingers and dropped them into the cupped-end. I saw him trace a triangle shape on the outside of the scoop, and the dried leaves burst into flame. Julian took care as he brought the scoop up to the glass spout and tapped the burning leaves into the sphere. Immediately the glass began to fill with a thick, dark smoke.

Julian set the tool back down onto the table and hunched forward, staring at the swirling smoke. A minute passed like this, then two. Wisps escaped through the spout into the air around us, singeing its way through my nose and making me feel light-headed. For one absurd moment I wondered whether Julian was old enough to be doing this sort of thing.

"What exactly are we doing?" I whispered to my companion.

Julian's head snapped up, he blinked in surprise as if he had forgotten my presence. "Oh. It shows you things. Answers, in the patterns of smoke." He turned back to his solemn study, mumbling, "Problem is figuring out what it means."

More captivated than ever, I leaned in next to the boy and gazed into the churning smoke with him. I worried for a fleeting second that I was being taken for a fool, but then the image began to take form. The currents of smoke turned on their axes and shifted around, rearranging into new shapes. I could make out a figure, a woman. She held a baby cradled in her arms. I stared, entranced, as the woman rocked the baby in her arms, the smoke swirling back and forth. Suddenly another figure, taller and broader than the first, materialized behind them and tipped its head down as if gazing at the baby in adoration. Then the smoke churned again and the image dissipated. I kept looking, waiting to see if I would be shown anything else. The gray clouds began to disperse, though, and eventually I was staring at nothing but smoldering embers in the bottom of a glass sphere.

I straightened, looked at Julian. "Did you see that, too?" I asked him, my voice brimming with wonder.

Julian lifted his shoulders in an offhand shrug. "Everyone sees something different," he told me. "We all have our own questions."

I digested that for a minute. What had my question been? I hadn't consciously been asking one. But subconsciously? I considered the possibility that the woman and child had been Cassandra and Wesley; it seemed the most obvious answer. If so, what was the smoke trying to show me about them? And who was the other figure, the man? After thinking on the matter for a while, I decided to let it go for the moment. I could feel the beginnings of a headache gathering behind my eyes.

"I'm done here," Julian said. "Are you?"

"Yeah," I uttered, rubbing my forehead. "Yeah. Wait. One more question. Those dates on the placards in front of the plants. What do those mean?"

Julian glanced over his shoulder at the host of plants lined behind him. "That's the year they started growing the plant. Not all of them are the originals, some were brought here as cuttings." He turned back to me to make sure I was following him. "The same changes that were made to our genes? To make us healthy and live longer? We try that stuff out on the plants first. We do other things to them too. Experiments."

I tried to absorb what he was telling me. The throbbing surged against the inside of my head, reminding me it was still there, clamoring for my attention. I grunted. "Okay. Let's blow this popsicle stand, shall we?" Julian gave me a look of such confusion that I laughed out loud. "I just mean, let's get the heck out of here."

Julian clapped his mouth shut and nodded. "Right. Come on." I was only too happy to comply.

Back in my own room, I determined a long, hot shower was in order. I let the stream of water pelt my shoulders, massaging stiff muscles. When I stepped out of the tub, the room was shrouded in steam.

I pulled on a pink pair of sweatpants and a camisole, swooped my hair up off my neck into a makeshift bun, and continued with my original plan of spending as much of the day as possible in my bedroom. I read, I dozed, I even did some yoga. My headache had faded, but the rumbling in my belly finally forced me to consider venturing out to get some dinner. But the thought of sitting at the same table as Jameson for an entire meal made me feel almost nauseous. I was struck with an idea: I would go to the bower. When Deborah arrived with Cassandra's tray of food, I would ask her to bring one for me as well.

Pleased with my plan, I got ready to go. A casual dinner with Cassandra in the bower wouldn't require getting dressed up, and so I decided what I was already wearing was good enough and left my room.

When I arrived at Cassandra's room I heard her speaking to someone. It wasn't the crooning she usually did when talking to the baby. I felt my stomach drop when I saw who else was sitting with her. I seriously considered backing right out of the room, but Cassandra had already heard my arrival and spotted me. "Anna!" she called out. "How perfect! You can join us for dinner, too!" I crossed the room reluctantly and took a seat. There across from me sat Jameson, leaning forward in his chair, elbows propped on his thighs, staring at where he held his hands clasped between his knees. One of his legs bounced up and down, his brow was drawn low over his eyes. He didn't look up at my arrival.

"Deborah should be here any time with our food. I'll send her to fetch some for you, too," Cassandra told me. I nodded. "I have just been trying to get my brother to tell me what has him in such a dismal mood. Perhaps you'll have more luck getting a serious answer out of him."

I doubted that very much. Before I had to make a reply, Wesley began to fuss and chew on his hands. "It's his dinnertime, too," Cassandra explained. "Excuse me for a moment. My son is not one for delaying gratification." I watched her get up from the sofa and cross over to the baby's crib. When I turned back, Jameson was looking at me. Not that he was making eye contact with me, but was rather appreciatively taking in my attire. I realized with mortification that I was basically wearing pajamas.

Cassandra returned and sat down. "Sorry. I'm afraid Wesley takes after the other Dorn men in some less desirable regards. They have little patience, if any. When they know what they want they take it, whether it's theirs to take or not." She tapped her son's nose affectionately and then spread the baby blanket she had retrieved over her chest in order to feed him discreetly.

I didn't tell Cassandra that I could personally attest to what she had just said. I snuck another glance at Jameson. Not surprisingly, he didn't have the grace to look embarrassed.

Unaware of my discomfort, Cassandra went on talking. "I can be very insistent myself, big brother. You were in such high spirits when you visited yesterday, and I want to know what has put you in such a foul mood."

I watched Jameson's whole upper body rise and then fall as he released a deep sigh. "Victor. What else?"

"You two always squabble," Cassandra observed.

"Not like this."

Cassandra's eyes searched her brother's face. "What were you fighting about?" Jameson tried to put an end to the line of questioning.

"Cassandra, must we-"

"What were you fighting about?" she repeated, her words clipped.

Jameson met his sister's gaze evenly. "If you must know...in broad terms, we were arguing about humans."

I felt myself grow cold all over. "You were arguing about me, weren't you?" I asked at the very same time that Cassandra said, "You were fighting about Grant, weren't you?"

Jameson looked from his sister to me and back again. "Yes and yes," he said. "Now may we please speak of something else?"

"Hold on a second," I argued. "If you're losing your battle to preserve my life here, I'd like to know about it. I think."

Jameson cast me a sober look. "Nothing has changed as far as that goes." The thought was not as comforting as one would hope.

"And Grant?" Cassandra asked, her voice breaking. Jameson wouldn't look at his sister when he answered.

"Nothing has changed. Victor was just on his usual rant about no good coming from interaction with humans, et cetera, et cetera. We argued as we always do, things just got a little more heated this time. You two have nothing to worry about. Nothing new, anyway." I saw Cassandra wipe at her eyes with the heel of her free hand. We each sat entangled in our own grim musings. Cassandra pulled Wesley out from under the blanket and coaxed a couple of burps from him, then rose to lay him in his crib.

Deborah bustled into the room at that moment, bearing two trays of food. As soon as she spied me, she immediately offered to bring another. Cassandra returned to her seat. She and Jameson waited politely for my dinner to arrive before eating their own. When Deborah returned and dropped off my dinner, we each started to pick at our food, lost in our own brooding thoughts. I think we had all lost our appetites. I snuck swift glances up at Jameson and Cassandra as we poked at our meals.

I was reflecting not only on my own predicament, but also how my presence was disrupting this family and even pitting them against one another. Strange that I should even concern myself with the well-being of these people who were, for all intents and purposes, my captors. But they weren't all so bad. Cassandra must have been thinking about this Grant person, who I could only assume was Wesley's father. Jameson was perhaps dwelling on all of these things. The next time I looked up, it was to find his eyes on me. Instead of the gravity that had been the theme of the evening up until that point, there was a heat behind his eyes. My pulse quickened in response.

We had been silent for so long that it startled me when Cassandra began speaking again. "You know, if Mother were still alive we wouldn't have to worry half so much about Victor."

Jameson turned to his sister, his eyes narrowed. "What do you mean?"

Cassandra didn't answer right away. Her cheeks flushed. I got the impression that what she was about to say was not easy for her. "At the Hakim's home, ten years ago, I snuck Evelyn out of bed so she could get a look at some of the celebrations that went on at night. The dancing, the light shows. When I told her it was time to get back we started to make our way to her room. We came across Mother and Nimra Hakim talking in the great hall. We hid so that we wouldn't get caught." Cassandra swallowed. Her eyes were far away. "They were talking about the motion they were going to propose at the meeting to overrule the tradition of the eldest child inheriting the leadership of the families that sit on the council. They thought it should be based on merit instead. Nimra mentioned her youngest son was best cut out for the job. Mother told her that she thought I would be the best choice for our family, but that certainly Victor was not suited for it." Cassandra shrugged and looked up. "Anyway, then she died and the meeting never happened. And Nimra didn't end up bringing it up at the next meeting either. So that was the end of that."

There was a pained look on Jameson's face. "You never told me that," he said, his voice faint. Cassandra shrugged again. "Like I said, it doesn't matter now."

After a moment, Jameson sat up straighter and rubbed his hands together. "Well, ladies, I do apologize for bringing everyone down with my mood this evening. Would have been better, I suppose, to keep to myself until it had passed. I just couldn't stomach the thought of sitting through dinner with that incorrigible brother of ours tonight." He sighed. "I think what I need is a distraction. Something to take my mind off all of this for a while. If you'll excuse me..." He nodded to both Cassandra and myself before leaving the room.

As soon as her brother was gone, Cassandra twisted around to face me and leaned over the arm of the sofa. "Anna. Can I ask you to do something for me?" Her tone was earnest, her voice low. Whatever she was about to bring up was something very important to her.

"Of course, Cassandra. What is it?"

"I..." She bit her bottom lip. "I hate to ask, but there's something I want very badly, and I was hoping you might get it for me."

"What is it?" I asked again.

"In the gardener's cottage there is a loose floorboard in the living room. It's underneath the little area rug. If you pry that up, you should find a small drawstring bag. I would be eternally grateful if you brought it to me."

I was intrigued. I was tempted to ask what was in the bag, but if Cassandra had wanted me to know, she would have told me. "Alright. The gardener's cottage. Is that what I took for a huge garden shed out there?"

"Yes. Part of it is for storing equipment, but that's also where Willow Glen's gardener stays. You'll have to go there sometime during the day when what's-his-name is busy outside. No one can see you doing this for me."

That part made me a bit nervous, knowing that this mission Cassandra was setting me on had the potential for landing me in more trouble than I already was. By the same token, though, the idea excited me. A small act of rebellion, demonstrating that the others in the family didn't have absolute control over me as they might like.

"Okay. I'll do it."

Cassandra smiled, but there was a tinge of sadness at the corners of her mouth. "Thank you, Anna. Thank you so much." She pulled away from me, sitting against the back of the couch. "And thanks for visiting. It's a pity it ended up being a sort of miserable evening. We had so much fun the last time the two of you visited." I wished her goodnight, and left her and her slumbering child to themselves.

I made the trek back toward my room. Collapsing into bed sounded like an amazing idea, and it was with that in mind that I turned my key in the lock and pushed the door open.

Jameson was in my room, gazing out the window with his hands in his pockets. He turned to face me. I flung the key onto the desktop with a clangor. "I don't know why I even bother with that thing," I said.

Jameson smiled at me wryly. "We know that for many humans, appearances-even false ones-can be comforting."

"Ah. Well it's good to know you all have my comfort in mind." I shifted my weight and placed my hands on my hips. My eyes flashed up and down his form. The sight of him brought such conflicting feelings, and I was confused. "To what do I owe this pleasure?"

He took a step toward me. "Is that venom I detect in your voice? As I recall, pleasure is exactly what you were expressing when I was here last night." Once again I felt the heat in my cheeks betray my reaction to his words. He closed the distance between us and looked down at me. "What, was I mistaken?"

I crossed my arms over my chest and said nothing, but the flush in my face was answer enough.

"What's the problem, then?"

I tried to put into words the way I had been feeling. I faltered, not sure if I would sound like a woman scorned, or a petulant child. "It's just that I hadn't been expecting...that sort of thing to happen. It took me by surprise. And then you just left without even saying a word, which I shouldn't have to tell you is a pretty shitty thing to do."

I could feel his breath on my skin, he was so close. "Have I ever done anything in our brief acquaintance that would have led you to believe I was the romantic type?"

I snorted with laughter. "No. Well, there was the stone. Flower. Crystal thingy."

"And when I gave that to you, I remember you saying I didn't have to try very hard to be an asshole." He was grinning lopsidedly as he spoke.

"Yeah, well. Still. There are rules of engagement in this sort of thing, even for practiced assholes."

"Were you hoping I would present you with bouquets and chocolates and handwritten haikus?"

I tried to picture a version of Jameson doing those things. "Well, I am rather fond of chocolate," I responded.

His face turned serious. "You say you hadn't been expecting it. Neither had I. I'm afraid I wasn't feeling quite myself last night. I apologize if I acted more of an asshole than usual. But in no way do I regret what happened. I quite enjoyed myself. And you?"

I was already tangled up in the awkwardness of the situation, and so decided I might as well jump in feet first. I held my chin high and refused to let my eyes waver from his when I answered. "As you already pointed out, I think it was obvious that I did."

"Then as two mature adults, why can't we enjoy what one another has to offer?"

A delicious tingling swept through my body. "No reason," I breathed.

"Good. I was hoping you would say that." Jameson slid a gentle hand under my chin and lowered his face so that our lips met. His other hand slithered up the back of my neck and raked through my hair, cupping the back of my head.

And just like that, the *eros* was rekindled.

As we lay recovering afterwards, my stomach growled and churned against Jameson's own.

He smiled widely.

"I couldn't have said it better myself. I couldn't help but notice that neither of us actually ate much at dinner." He pushed himself into a sitting position, lifting me in the process. I reluctantly pulled myself off of him and kneeled on the bed next to him. Jameson stepped down to the floor and began putting his clothes back on. I shouldn't have been surprised that he was leaving so soon again. I watched as he got himself dressed, stared at the rippling muscles of his bare back until a he tugged his shirt over it.

While he buckled his belt, Jameson half-turned to face me. "Are you going to get dressed, or will you be accompanying me naked? Not that I would mind. Please, feel free to remain as you are."

"Accompany you? Where are we going?"

"Why, to raid the kitchen, of course."

I dressed hurriedly and followed right behind Jameson as we left my room and descended the grand staircase. The place was dark and empty. It seemed everyone else had already retired for the night.

Once in the kitchen, Jameson walked directly to the refrigerator and opened it, leaning in and perusing the shelves. "Do you care for strawberries?" he asked.

"I love strawberries."

He set a carton half full of the fruit on the counter between us and we fell silent for a time as we both set to eating. Juice dribbled down my chin and I wiped at it with a finger. Jameson lunged and grabbed hold of my hand. "Allow me," he said, taking my finger into his mouth and sucking the juice off. I rolled my eyes, but smiled.

Together we finished the remaining strawberries. I watched bewildered as Jameson closed the empty carton and placed it back into the refrigerator. "I like to keep Deborah guessing," he gave as way of explanation. He then began rifling through one of the cupboards. "Ah, here we are," he said as he drew out a bar of chocolate. Unwrapping it, he said, "I know how very fond you are of chocolate." He took a great bite out of the bar before handing the rest of it to me.

"How very chivalrous of you, Mr. Dorn," I observed.

"Just don't let anyone else hear you say that." I bit off a piece of the chocolate while he chewed his own. He let out a grunt of satisfaction. "This night ended up improving more than I could have ever hoped. But now, if you'll excuse me, I regrettably have some work I must attend to."

"Work? At this hour? What kind of work?" I asked.

"There are still preparations to be made."

"Preparations for what?"

He searched my eyes. "No one has told you about the council meeting yet? It's being held here at Willow Glen this time. I can tell you more some other time. Right now there is work that needs to be done, and I have procrastinated long enough. Although you really are a most delightful distraction." He leaned in for one last searing kiss, sweetened by the taste of strawberries and chocolate. And then I was alone.

8

July 30th, 2013

Today I realized I was running short on cat food. I had been putting off grocery shopping for myself, but Dinah would likely never forgive me if I allowed a lapse in her feeding schedule. Plus, I had sworn that I would get myself away from Willow Glen Manor and into the real world, just for a little while. For my sanity's sake. The idea of going out made me anxious, though. It seemed an eternity had passed since I had been among those who continued going about their lives of routine without even an inkling of the things I had come to know.

It felt strange to be driving my car for the first time since arriving at Willow Glen. Otherwise the trip into town was uneventful. Once I was in the grocery store surrounded by other shoppers, however, I felt like a foreigner immersed in an unfamiliar culture. I couldn't help but stare at everything and everyone around me, frightened and fascinated at the same time. These were *humans!* There were so many of them. I felt awkward in their midst, but at the same time I had the mad urge to run up to each and every one of them and shake them by the shoulders, yelling, "Do you have any idea what has been happening to me? The things I have learned?"

I purchased enough food for the cat and myself to keep me from having to make another trip any time soon. Once home, I gave Dinah a treat of canned food and fixed a sandwich for myself. The cat wolfed her meal down and then set out to do whatever it is she likes to do on her own in this vast house, leaving me feeling absurdly lonesome. I finished my own lunch and then decided it was time to continue writing down my story.

The next morning I began my routine as usual, looking in on Nathaniel, hopeful that maybe the treatment Evelyn had mixed up had begun to improve her grandfather's health. I had to take only one look at him, though, to see that he was only getting sicker. His legs had become obscenely swollen; my fingertips left indentations when I touched the cool, shiny skin of his feet to feel for pulses. All I could do was suggest he keep them elevated as much as possible.

"You drank the medicine?" I asked after lifting my stethoscope from the wet sounds of his breathing.

"Mmm," Nathaniel said in response. I almost felt like shaking the man, pointing out that a noncommittal noise was hardly an answer, and offering to give him a lollipop if he took his medicine like a good boy. I chided myself after having those thoughts; in the field of healthcare we can teach people tips about how to best take care of themselves, but we can't force them to make the decisions we would choose for them. It was just frustrating to watch your patient decline and feel there was nothing more you could do to stop it. Nathaniel spoke again, though, adding, "Stuff hardly had a taste to it at all, thankfully. Alas…" He made a sweeping gesture with his hands, encompassing his entire body at once.

I felt a sinking feeling in my chest, but did my best to hide it. "Well, maybe it just takes a while to have an effect?" I hadn't meant for it to come out as a question.

Nathaniel gave me a knowing look. We wrapped up the rest of our visit as usual. My appeals for getting outside help were once again disregarded.

When I took my leave of Nathaniel, I lingered for a time in his sitting room. I spent a solid few minutes staring at the portrait of the late Vivienne Dorn, then sauntered around the room pretending to admire the furnishings and decor. I craned my neck to peek around the frame of the sliding glass doors. I could see Nathaniel's outstretched legs. There was no movement I could detect, but I couldn't be sure if he had nodded off.

Instead of making my way to Cassandra's room next, I skipped down the grand staircase, through the kitchen, and out the back door. I squinted against the bright rays of the sun. At first glance, the gardener's whereabouts weren't obvious. I stepped down from the terrace and tried to appear as if out for one of my casual strolls through the gardens. As I walked, I cast about looking for Tom. Doubling around one of the hedges by the gazebo on the grounds, I came across him at his work. His gloved hands were wrapped around the wooden handles of a wheelbarrow, which he was pushing my way.

"Morning!" he called out when he caught sight of me.

"Good morning," I answered, side-stepping out of his path. I watched him keep going on past the gazebo and toward the back perimeter of the gardens. That was about as far as he could get from the cottage, a fact for which I was grateful.

Turning, I shielded my eyes with a hand and snuck a look up at the main house. I could make out Nathaniel's form sitting out on his balcony. From that distance, I still couldn't tell if he was asleep or not. I would have to be careful when I made my move to enter the cottage.

I lowered my head as I tramped toward the outbuilding, apparently going for the "if I can't see you, you can't see me" approach. I slowed as I neared the structure that acted as both storage for tools and residence for the gardener. The door was on the side facing the main house. I glanced quickly at Nathaniel again, but there was no way to know for sure if he was watching me. I paused, not sure how to proceed. The sound of insects humming seemed to intensify as I hesitated. I felt a coat of sweat break out on my skin.

I decided to circle around the back of the building and see what things look like there. With a jolt of satisfaction, I saw there were windows in the back. The glass panes were slid open, with only screens in place. The fleeting delight wilted when I realized that I might have no way of getting the screens open from the outside. "Damn," I said under my breath.

Without any other bright ideas forthcoming, I approached the nearest window and slid my fingernails into the crack between the screen and the window's casement. Curling my fingers, I tugged. The edge of the screen shifted slightly, but that was all. I placed my other hand above the first one, digging those nails in as well. I braced myself and then jerked, hard, and with a satisfying popping noise, the screen came free and clattered to the ground. I froze at the loud noise. Willing myself to move, I looked over my shoulder to make sure I hadn't attracted any unwanted attention. Nobody materialized as I half-feared they would, and I breathed a sigh of relief. "I guess it's about time my luck changed."

The cottage was a single story and the windows were low enough that I could heave myself up and swing my legs over. I slipped through feet first, my neck extended back like in a game of limbo. My shoes met the solid floor, my chin grazed by the edge of the window's opening, and I straightened up, now inside the gardener's home. My pulse was thrumming in my veins. I wanted to get the job over and done with as quickly as possible.

I had to take a minute to let my eyes adjust to the relative dimness of the interior. Once they did, I saw that I was inside a kitchenette area. Two doors led off of the room, and through one I could see the rumpled form of an unmade bed. I turned to the other opening and strode through.

I found myself in the living area Cassandra had mentioned. Spotting the little rug right away, I hurried over to it and squatted to the floor. I grabbed at the rug, pulling it aside in a bunched up heap. I eyed the floorboards beneath. There was none that I could tell was loose from just looking. Picking one at random, I began to try to lift each board at the corner, searching for the right one through process of elimination.

The only problem was, none of them so much as budged beneath my fingers.

I tried each floorboard again, thinking maybe I had just missed something. Still, none moved. I rolled back onto my heels and exhaled, wiping a damp strand of hair from my face. I tried to think what to do next.

Was it possible the rug had been moved to a different spot since the last time Cassandra had been in the gardener's cottage? How often would she have found herself there, anyway? I had no idea, but my eyes skimmed over the other exposed floorboards in the room. I stood to get a better view, and right away something caught my eye. Over by a coffee table and a recliner, the patterned wood of the floor was disrupted. A small piece was missing from the corner of one of the boards, leaving ragged edges. Daring to hope, I stepped over and crouched down, hooking my finger into the crater and pulling. The floorboard tilted up without any resistance.

Just beneath the surface of the floor was the drawstring bag Cassandra had said would be there. A satiny gray pouch, about the size of my hand. I scooped it out of the hollow I had revealed, then lowered the board back into place. "Gotcha."

I could feel the weight of the bag's contents through the thin material. Whatever was inside was firm, heavy. My curiosity was piqued. Pushing away the urge to look inside, I turned my attention to making my getaway. Thankfully, I had the presence of mind to smooth the rug back in its place before hurrying to the window and shimmying my way back out of the cottage. I slid the screen back onto its track, heard it snap into place. Then I high-tailed it back to the main house, my prize clutched in a sweaty and trembling hand.

I made right for Cassandra's room. When I entered I held the bag up for her to see. As soon as she saw what I had in my hand her face crumpled and silent tears began to spill, but she was smiling. She held out her arms, eager for my delivery, and I dropped the pouch into her waiting hands.

"Thank you so, so much," she said to me between shaking breaths. She held the bag up to her cheek and closed her eyes. I felt my own eyes begin to sting out of sympathy, and I didn't even know what it was were be crying about. I sniffed, chasing back the infectious tears. It was plain that, whatever that bag was, it meant the world to Cassandra to have it in her possession. I was glad to have helped.

A couple of days passed after stealing into the gardener's cottage. Nathaniel's health was only getting worse with time. There hadn't been any opportunities to see Jameson other than at dinnertime and for *digestifs* afterwards, where he seemed disinclined to explain more to me about the council meeting in front of the others. There was evidence of the preparations for the upcoming gathering all over the house. They had opened up the ballroom, the servants never seemed to stop scurrying around. I heard talk of a string quartet and a feast, of a masqued ball with a peacock theme, whatever that might mean. I was mostly overlooked in all of the commotion.

As much as I might have preferred to take all of my meals in Cassandra's room, I didn't want to seem discourteous. I assumed my place at the dining room table most nights. I actually felt a slight pang of sympathy for Zahira, knowing that she had spent years enduring these tense dinners with a family who seemed to butt heads incessantly.

"I hope you are finding ways to enjoy your stay here at Willow Glen, Miss Cassidy," Nathaniel said one evening, after he was seated and had taken the time to catch his breath. I was sipping some of my water when he asked and it took me a moment to respond. Jameson turned in his seat and raised his eyebrows at me, waiting for my answer. I couldn't suppress a giggle and ended up spluttering into my glass. I faked a cough in a lame attempt to cover up my blunder. "Um, yes. Yes, I have been made to feel most comfortable. Thank you."

"Comfortable, eh?" Jameson asked. I ignored him.

"Miss Cassidy's comfort is not exactly our primary concern with her stay here, is it?" Victor bit out.

Nathaniel shook his head wearily. "Victor, in your obsession with our family's position of authority, you forget that courtesy also goes a long way in maintaining influence. As long as she is here, no matter what the reason, it only adds to the honor of our family name by making her feel welcome."

"I welcome her presence here," Jameson chipped in.

Nathaniel gestured toward his younger son with a wilting hand. "See? You might actually learn something from your brother sometimes, Victor."

"Not likely," Victor scoffed.

"You could each learn something from the other, as a matter of fact."

"Doubt it," Jameson retorted.

Matters didn't improve during drinks in the drawing room. After downing some of his brandy, Nathaniel smacked his lips and wiped away the beads of perspiration that had collected on his forehead. "I can't wait until this whole council meeting business is over and done with."

"Whyever would you say that?" Victor wanted to know. "These gatherings with the other great families on the council present some of our best moments of opportunity."

"Usually this is a great chance to confer with the others, yes, but you know why I am dreading this one. If they were to learn the full extent of my illness, or worse yet, about what has happened with your sister...Besides, amongst the good people of the Sentient are plenty of dithering, arrogant fools who have forgotten the very tenets we are supposed to uphold."

Victor frowned. "You should not insult them so. Some of these people have made the greatest discoveries of our time."

"Such as Zahira's cousin learning how to accidentally set himself on fire," Jameson interjected. This earned him a fierce glare from his sister-in-law.

"This reminds me," Victor said in response, "little brother, do try to hide your true vexing nature while we play host to the other families, would you? It is imperative we make a good impression. In fact," here Victor leaned forward in his seat, "as a young and eligible bachelor, you may actually have the potential to be of use to this family for once. Alain and Marie Valois will be here with their daughter Genevieve. I don't need to explain to you that they are one of the most illustrious families among the Sentient."

Jameson tilted his head back. "Ah, so you hope to marry me off and ship me to France to get me out of your hair. Perhaps I should aspire to get the young lady with child while she is here, so her parents have no choice but accept me into their illustrious family?"

Victor curled his upper lip. "Who you marry and who you choose to stick your dick into are little concern of mine."

"*Victor!*" Zahira said with a sharp intake of breath. Julian's face reddened at his father's words, while Evelyn tried to maintain a studied look of indifference.

"I simply wish you would charm the lady while she is here, keep her entertained. She can then tell her parents what a decent sort the Dorns are."

Nathaniel joined the conversation. "We may have different reasons, but I think I agree with your brother here. I do not want to risk anyone learning of our family's...disgrace. We should be as hospitable as possible, and anything we can do to keep our guests amused and *distracted* would be beneficial. Perhaps a little flirtation is not out of order, if that's what it takes."

"The things I do for family," Jameson said before draining his liquor. I tipped back my own glass and when I resurfaced I met his eyes. The brandy burned a path down my throat and into the pit of my stomach, and I felt a fire ignite even deeper within my body. The look Jameson was giving me told me that, preparations or no, he would be stopping by later that night.

As it turns out, I hadn't even reached my room yet when, as I passed a dissecting hallway, a hand reached out and clasped my shoulder.

I gasped. "Jesus, Jameson!"

His eyes glinted with amusement. "So sorry. But you do look so very pretty when you're terrified."

"You once told me that my awkwardness when I first arrived here was amusing. And now my terror attracts you? How..."

"Unromantic? I thought we already covered this topic."

I laughed, despite the fact that my heart was still pounding in my throat. Jameson's hand shifted until it was cradling the back of my neck. He leaned in closer.

"The other families will be arriving soon. There are eight altogether, including us; the heads of the households plus whichever other family members they choose to sit with them at the council meeting. They will be bringing some of their own servants to assist ours during the coming days when there will be so many more people than usual to see to. Anyone who sees you will just assume you are a servant of one of the other families. Since my father wishes us to pretend nothing out of the ordinary has happened, Cassandra must put in an appearance so as not to raise suspicions. You will be kept in her room at those times, to watch the baby."

I bristled at the word "kept," but realized he was only trying to warn me what to expect.

"Alright. Thanks for letting me know."

His hand slid off my neck and he traced a light finger down my spine. He then slipped his hand into mine and started in the direction of my room. I dug my heels in, holding my place.

Jameson turned around and shot me a questioning look.

"I've just decided," I told him. "You're taking me on a date."

His eyebrows arched. "I am? Splendid. Where am I taking you?"

"To the ballroom. I've never been in a genuine ballroom before."

Jameson stepped closer to me again. "I see. I think you'll be impressed. It's very...room-like. Just wait until you see its rectangular shape, its four walls."

"Just take me there, would you?"

"As the lady commands."

We slipped back down the stairs and Jameson led me to the ballroom, throwing open the great double doors.

Our steps echoed in the cavernous room. A sparkling chandelier suspended from the ceiling, and an enormous mirror graced the wall at one end, making the ballroom look even bigger than it was.

"You're right," I said, coming to a stop in the middle of the room. "I'm impressed."

"It's the four walls, isn't it?"

I ignored him and approached the wall across from the entrance, which was covered with a mural depicting a nighttime woodland scene. The bright orb of the moon hung in one corner of the painting, brought to life with brush strokes of varying shades and intensity, giving the illusion of craters and ridges. Trees, grasses and stones were bathed in the white luster of moonlight. In the center was a tree different from the others. It loomed in the forefront, thick and sturdy, with leaves that were illumined with a more yellowish tint than the rest of the picture, as if lit from within. Plump, golden fruit weighed down its branches. So lifelike was the artwork that my mouth practically watered at the sight of them. The bark of the tree was patterned in a way that hinted at human faces up and down its length. Striking, inscrutable, knowing faces.

"Actually," I said, my voice hushed with wonder, "the walls *are* pretty amazing."

Pairs of glowing eyes were shown clustered around the tree, fauna peering through branches or from inside logs. I felt Jameson draw up next to me. He pointed to these watchful eyes and said, "Those are actually the souls of our enemies throughout the ages, trapped forever for crossing us."

"Bullshit."

He chuckled. "I like that about you. You always see through my bullshit, and aren't afraid to call me on it."

I held a hand out toward the mural. "So, this forest scene. The woodland creatures, the glowy tree. It's unbelievably gorgeous and all, but-are you sure you guys aren't really fairies or something?"

I didn't get an answer, but I could feel the disapproval surging my way. I smirked, not taking my eyes from the wall. "Yeah, this is definitely something you would find in a fairy's house."

"I'll let that slide, because I agree it's a bit melodramatic. The one who commissioned this painting fancied mixing together a few ideologies, as it suited him. Elixir of life, tree of life, tree of knowledge. A race of perfect beings as the fruit borne of it all. Sometimes referred to as ambrosia: the fruit of the gods."

"Gods, huh?"

"You can't rush perfection, sweetheart. Give us another generation or two to nail it. Besides, I told you how I feel about all of that nonsense. It may have begun with admirable ideas, but now it's not much more than archaic drivel from the mouths of those who seek to maintain their positions of power."

I could tell from the edge in his voice that this was a topic Jameson found distasteful. I didn't think dropping another dig about fairies would go over well. Instead, I pivoted away from the wall to get a better look at the rest of the ballroom. The floor gleamed with the reflections of twinkling lights from the chandelier above.

"Dance with me," Jameson said, surprising me.

I shook my head. "I don't dance."

Jameson clasped my elbow and turned me to face him. He lowered both hands to my hips and began to try to steer my body to match his own swaying movements. I resisted, holding myself rigid. Jameson bent in closer to look me in the eye. "Dance with me, Anna. Or I swear, I'll keep you my prisoner and force you to do my bidding, and your little kitty, too."

I couldn't suppress a burst of laughter. "What's new?" I gave in, though, placing my hands on his shoulders and allowing him to lead me in a slow turning around the floor. I'm not sure how long it took, but eventually I stopped noticing the lack of music playing, forgot my discomfort with dancing. I let my mind dissolve into my body until all that was left was an awareness of the motion, the back and forth, the solid warmth of him beneath my hands and his own hands on my waist. His thumbs traced light circles on the sensitive flesh in front of my hip bones, teasingly, setting my stomach muscles to trembling. I think we went on like that for a while.

At first, neither of us noticed the footsteps. Then there was Deborah, walking through the open doors with her arms full of cleaning supplies. She froze when she saw us. We leapt apart from one another as soon as we saw her.

It was hard to tell who was more mortified. The housekeeper said nothing, but her eyes looked about to burst from her skull.

"Good evening, Deborah," Jameson called out after a moment of stunned silence. He gestured to the cargo in her arms. "Keep up the good work," he said, right before grabbing my hand in his and dashing for the doors.

Once in the great hall, I folded my arms over my stomach and bent over giggling. Jameson laughed under his breath. "I feel like a teenager again, sneaking around to not get caught by my parents," he said.

When I could breathe again, I straightened up and said, "Consider it practice. For when one of the cousins comes up with a way to reverse the aging process, and you really are a teen again.

"Heaven help me," Jameson beseeched. "Once was bad enough. I don't think you would care for me, the way I was as a teenager."

"What makes you think I care for you now?" I challenged.

Jameson crooked an eyebrow at me. "I can outline the reasons, but you'll only just blush again." He took my hand again. "I know this is our first date and all, but would you think less of me if I asked you to stay the night?"

"Well, it would be the first time you've *asked* anything of me, and so I would call that an improvement."

"Then I know the perfect way to wrap up the night."

"Oo la la," I teased. "And what, exactly, would that be?"

"I was thinking along the lines of a rousing match of chess in the drawing room," he joked.

Our eager footsteps didn't take us to the drawing room, though, but up the grand staircase and to my bedroom once again.

In the days that followed I felt like a hindrance, always in someone's way. I spent more time with Cassandra, who at least seemed to appreciate the company. One day I wandered into the kitchen. Deborah was busy at the sink. I have always been pretty hopeless in a kitchen, but I wanted to try to make myself useful and so I asked the housekeeper if there was anything I could do to help.

"Oh, if you could just take the tray of vegetables out to the table for me. The first family arrived today. We wouldn't want them not to have anything to peck at. It's right here in the fridge." Deborah tugged the refrigerator door open to point me to the tray. Her eyebrows drew together and she leaned forward, standing back up with the empty strawberry carton in her hand.

"Looks like that scoundrel Tom has been helping himself again."

"Tom." I had to reach into my mind to place the name. "The gardener?"

Deborah nodded. "Friendly enough fellow, but this wouldn't be the first time he's lifted things from the house." Her eyes widened and she turned to look me full in the face. "Nothing valuable, mind you. Nothing to bother the master about. I wouldn't want to lose another..."

"Don't worry, Deborah. If you don't want them to know, I certainly won't be the one to tell them."

The housekeeper's face immediately relaxed, and she waved me on. "Bless your heart. I'd be grateful if you could just put those snacks out for me. Then why don't you go outside and enjoy the gorgeous day? Since none of the rest of us can just now."

With nothing better to do, I took Deborah's advice and went out through the back door onto the terrace. A few wispy clouds scudded across the brilliant sky. It was warm out, but with a caressing breeze. Birdsong drifted through the air and from somewhere amidst the greenery I could hear the gardener at work.

I hopped down the steps and started down the path. The pond in one of the far corners seemed a good a place as any to pass the time.

Willow Glen Manor boasted a koi pond that was considerably larger than those that could be found in the average suburban backyard. The pool extended far enough that a small stone bridge arched from one side to the other. As I drew near, I was surprised to see that someone else was already there. A young man stood in the center of the bridge, gazing down into the water.

It was someone I had never laid eyes on before. He had black curly hair that grew so that it stood out from his head a bit, but not long enough to cover his ears. He was slender but looked fit; the muscle of his bronzed arms where they extended beneath his sleeves was well-defined. His eyes, when he looked up at my approach, were enormous and brown, framed by long black lashes. I hadn't noticed that he had been listening to music until he popped the buds out of his ears and shoved his iPod down into his jeans pocket. He offered me a gentle smile and said "Hello."

At a guess I would have put him at about twenty years old. In Sentient years, I couldn't have said. "Oh. Hi. I'm sorry, I didn't mean to disturb you-"

He was shaking his head. "Please. Disturb me. I'm kind of bored out of my skull after traveling for so long." His eyes swept over me, assessing. "You work here?" he asked.

"I...I..." I hadn't been prepared for meeting any of the others yet! If only one of the families had arrived so far, it wasn't possible for me to pretend to just be someone else's servant. And if I said I worked for the Dorns, what could I claim my role was? I certainly didn't look dressed for any sort of position in the household, in my own jeans and embroidered top with spaghetti straps.

The young man actually looked pained at my discomfort, one side of his face pulled up into a grimace. Before I could muster any sort of reply he stepped in and saved me from having to make any. He extended a hand to me. "I'm Reza," he told me. "Hakim."

I recognized the last name. "My name is Anna," I said, shaking his hand. "I do know that much." He tipped his head back slightly and laughed, a sound that rang out over the surface of the pond and took me aback with its natural fervor.

"There are so few things in this world we can be sure of," he replied. "Knowing who we are is an important one."

"In that case," I said as I withdrew my hand from his. "I don't think I'm doing so hot."

He cast his eyes over me again, this time with a more probing gaze. He apparently found what he had been looking for and said, "Nah, you're gonna be alright." He turned and leaned back over onto the bridge's balustrade. "Some of us just take longer than others to find the right path."

"I don't know if I'm even on the map anymore."

I could see the corner of his mouth lift. "I think you're closer than you realize."

Just then the gardener came into view with his shears and set to work on some shrubs at the far end of the pond. We watched him for a time.

"So who else is here with you?" I asked after a while.

"My parents and my brother Omar. My oldest brother stayed at home this time, with his tail tucked between his legs."

Things clicked into place in my head. "Is he the one who accidentally set himself on fire?"

Reza laughed again. "The one and the same. He wasn't actually injured too badly; my dad was in the lab with him and they put the flames out right away. It's his pride that's hurt more than anything."

"And where exactly is home?" I wanted to know.

"Marrakesh."

"Ah. You're Moroccan?" I could only detect the faintest hint of an accent, and it was not one I could place.

"We're originally from Turkey, actually," he answered. "We still have a home there, but these days we spend most of our time at our place in Marrakesh."

"I see." Truthfully, in my mind I was thinking about how different life must be when you had homes all over the world, when you could just move to a different country on a whim. I wasn't surprised, though. If Jameson could fashion a crystal flower out of an ordinary stone, and since one of the main precepts of historical alchemy was the endeavor to turn base materials into gold, I was sure accumulating wealth was not a problem for any of the Sentient.

We could hear the sound of the gardener humming to himself as his voice skimmed across the water to where we stood. We watched as he did a little jig and actually jumped to clap his heels together. "Dude really loves his work," Reza noted. Tom then lifted the flap of his breast pocket and pulled out a silver flask. Tossing his head back he helped himself to a lengthy swig. "Ah, that's why so happy," Reza said.

"Tsk tsk," I added. Then, "Well, it was nice to meet you, but I guess I'll be heading back inside now."

"Okay. See you around, Anna." I started making my way back toward the house. At one point I turned around for one last glimpse of my new acquaintance. He hadn't replaced his ear buds. He still stood leaning over the edge of the stone bridge, his shirt stretching up and revealing an expanse of golden skin and the band of his boxers peeking out above his pants. He was certainly not what I had expected to find in another Sentient. His eyes were fixed on the pond, his gaze as penetrating as if he could read secrets in the water below.

I left with an extra spring in my step, a buoyancy in my spirit that hadn't been there for some time. I can't say why, but when Reza Hakim told me I was going to be alright, I believed him.

9

July 31st, 2013

Is it possible to miss someone you barely got to know? Is it truly the person you miss, or your idea of who they are?

I've never been one to believe in fate, but recent events have me half-convinced that there are some people who come into your life for a reason. They show up exactly when you need them the most, even though you never realized you were in need.

Apparently I wax philosophical when I spend too much time by myself. And with the cat. Time to work on telling more of my story, to keep myself from dwelling too much on things that can't be changed.

When I returned to my room for the night, there was a thin white box laid out on my desk, a dark blue ribbon tied around it. Once again, I had left my door locked when I was out, but once again, it hadn't mattered. Someone had been in to leave this…gift, was it? I had a guess who it might have been. Someone brazen enough to let himself into my room uninvited, and who might wish to present me with something other than insults or death.

My curiosity piqued, I pried off the lid off of the box. Inside, nestled on a bed of cotton, was a bracelet made of linking plates of some polished black stone shot through with veins of red. I plucked the piece of jewelry up in my fingers and lifted it in front of my face for a better look.

"Careful," I murmured. "Someone could mistake this for a romantic gesture." I can't say I wasn't pleased, though. I slipped the bracelet over my wrist and admired it.

A minute passed, and then a soft knock came at my door. I mentally shook myself for acting like such a smitten girl. I let my arm drop and answered the door.

If I was expecting a specific person, I was surprised to see that it was Julian come to my room. He looked up at me from the doorway. "Can I play with Dinah for a little while?" he asked. I felt like the mother to some school aged child, *can Dinah come out to play?* The thought warmed me.

"Sure," I told the boy, stepping to the side so that he could enter.

Julian didn't budge. He was staring with a fearful look on his face, much like he used to always look around me when I first came to his family's home. Only this time his eyes weren't aimed at my face. I followed his gaze. When I lifted my arm, the one with the bracelet around the wrist, his eyes lifted to follow it.

"Where did you get that?" he whispered. He was scaring me.

"I found waiting for me here in my room. Why? Julian, what is it?"

The boy lunged forward with an uncharacteristic boldness and grasped onto my arm. He slid the bracelet over my hand and off of me. I gasped when I saw what was revealed.

My skin beneath where the bracelet had touched was an unhealthy shade of gray, shriveled and puckered. Alarm churned my stomach and the taste of bile flooded the back of my throat. I brought my wrist up for a closer look and turned my arm around, horrified. "Oh my god!"

Julian marched past me and to my desk. He dropped the bracelet back into its box and fitted its lid over top. "I'll get rid of it for you," he told me, swallowing hard. He was just as unnerved as I was. Well, maybe not quite as much-he wasn't the one whose flesh appeared to have decayed within a matter of minutes. I shoved the door shut and crossed to where he stood, inspected his fingertips where he had touched the jewelry. They were unchanged. "It won't work on me," he explained.

"What *is* it?" I breathed.

Julian gave me a look that was almost pitying. "Someone played a nasty trick on you."

"You think?" I gathered the courage to run the fingers of my hand over the desiccated skin, assessing the damage. "Is it going to spread?" My voice was shrill with panic.

Julian shook his head vehemently in an effort to reassure me. "Not as long as you don't put it back on. I don't think that will last, either. You must not have had it on for very long, otherwise" He cut off, leaving me to guess what the result would have been, and how quickly it would have arrived. He pointed to my wrist. "See? It's already getting better."

I stared at the band of rotten flesh and, after a long moment of suspense, saw that he was right. Already the gray was starting to fade, the skin was beginning to plump back up and smooth itself out. I dropped into my desk chair and refused to take my eyes away until the repair was complete. In the awkward silence that ensued while I waited and watched, Julian walked over to where Dinah had been sitting on her haunches by the armoire and began to pet her. He ran his fingers along the floor. She followed them with enormous pupils, her hindquarters shaking as she prepared to attack.

In a matter of minutes it seemed the damage to my wrist had been completely erased. I watched Julian play with the cat for several minutes, darting looks back down at my arm every so often to make sure it was still okay. I was no longer in the mood for company, but could hardly turn the boy away after he had just, in effect, saved me. Would the mystery bracelet have killed me, or just rendered me hideous to look at for the rest of my days? Neither was a fate I cared to meet. I was extremely grateful that he had shown up right when he did. I berated myself: that had been way too close for comfort, and a reminder that I wasn't just a houseguest staying with family friends. Perhaps I had been getting a little too comfortable in my situation.

Julian noticed the shift in my mood. He still seemed unsettled, as well. He gave Dinah one last pat on the head and walked back over to me. I kept a wary eye on the box as he scooped it up from my desk and pocketed it. "I'll put this back," he reiterated.

I tore my eyes from the box to look Julian in the eye. "Put it back? You know where it came from?" I remembered, suddenly, the display cabinet in the secret room with all of the plants and lab equipment. I had seen different pieces of jewelry inside, along with other baubles that had seemed out of place. Could that be where this bracelet had come from?

Julian fidgeted. "There's a collection of these things," he said to his feet. "I knew what they were for, but…I don't think we ever actually used them before." He shrugged. "Least not that I know of."

I had the feeling that there were plenty of things this boy's family had done that he was not aware of. Otherwise, how could he still be so sweet? I didn't want to make him any more uncomfortable, finding himself caught in between me and his own blood, and so I stood up and gave his shoulder a reassuring squeeze. "Thank you," I told him, my voice full of feeling.

"Welcome," Julian said softly. He gave a little wave of his hand and then left.

My nerves were in overdrive and I wasn't sure how I was going to be able to fall asleep any time soon. What had all of that been about, then? Another reminder to keep me in my place? Or something more dire? Either way, I made a mental note to not accept any more unmarked gifts while living among the Dorns.

Other Sentient families filtered in over the next two days. I kept to my own room as much as I could. Not only did I want to stay out of the way to avoid uncomfortable questions, but I was on edge after what had happened with the bracelet. Had I begun to actually feel comfortable amidst my captors? I would have to keep in mind that, no matter how well I might think I liked some of the family, I still had enemies at Willow Glen. The entire manor house was bustling with activity those days, and I didn't have an opportunity alone with Jameson to tell him about what had happened. I kept a close eye on everyone, especially Victor, to see if I could catch a look of surprise at seeing me unwithered and relatively well. There were no obvious reactions. Those who usually glared at me glared still, and the same was true with those who mostly ignored me or who made nice. I made a show of smiling a lot, to pretend that I was unfazed, and a worthier opponent than they may have guessed.

When I did venture out of my room, I took to wearing black dress slacks and nice blouses so that if anyone saw me during the times I did step out into the house, at least I looked more the part of a servant.

The afternoon came when Frederick showed up at my bedroom door and instructed me to follow him. "Miss Cassandra is expected at the ball tonight," he explained. "You are needed in her chambers." I nodded tersely, said goodbye to Dinah, and accompanied the butler to the bower.

Cassandra was in a silk robe applying makeup at her vanity. She was making an extra effort to cover the puffy circles I spied beneath her reddened eyes. "I'll nurse Wesley just before I go," she told me without turning around. "That should keep him sated for at least a few hours. He usually falls asleep by nine. I always rock him in my arms for a while before putting him in his crib."

"Okay," I said. I noticed the tears begin to spill over her cheeks again. She groaned in exasperation, snatched up a tissue and dabbed furiously at her face before reapplying her cover up.

I held the baby and cooed at him while his mother continued to get herself ready for that evening's affair. I offered my help but there was not much I could do until an hour or so later when she was ready to step into her dress and asked me to zip up the back. It was a one-shouldered navy blue gown with an empire waist to hide the roundness of her belly that remained from having delivered her baby so recently. Her auburn tresses were swept up off of her neck, showcasing dangling diamond earrings. She was even more stunning than usual.

Cassandra twirled around and we faced each other. "I don't plan on staying too long," she said. "Just long enough to be seen looking alive."

I could sense the tears resurfacing and held out a hand. "Do *not* cry! You'll just have to fix your make-up again," I warned, appealing to her practical side. From experience, I knew that sympathy often only made it harder to maintain control.

Cassandra sucked in a long, shuddering breath and composed herself. "At least I have this," she said, opening a box on her vanity and lifting an object out of the folds of glittery tissue paper inside. I saw that it was a mask, black studded with crystals that flashed in the light. It was more like a half-mask, really; when Cassandra fitted it to her face it covered only her eyes and nose, leaving her mouth free. "I can even wear it at dinner, so if I do breakdown at least no one will be the wiser." Her eyes were luminous as they met mine from behind her mask. "Take good care of him, Anna," she whispered.

"Of course. We'll be fine. See you in a while."

Cassandra grabbed her handbag from where it had been tossed onto the bed, and then left her room for the first time since returning home with her son.

Time passed slowly. I tried to imagine everything that was going on downstairs: the feast, the music and dancing, drinks out on the terrace. Wesley was contented for the most part. When he began to fuss at one point I distracted him by bouncing him gently in my arms and carrying him over to look out the window. As usual, the garden was lit up with the glowing orbs suspended in the foliage. The fountain was somehow alight as well, its shimmering waters changing color every so often. I could make out the forms of a few people here and there, mingling amidst the foliage.

When the time came, I put Wesley to bed as instructed and sat tucked in a corner of the sofa, waiting. I had about an hour alone with my churning thoughts before the door pushed open and Cassandra stepped back into the room. She looked drained. She gave me a half-smile, pulled the mask from her face and slipped out of her shoes, padding across the room to look into the crib. After watching her son sleep for a time she stole over to the sitting area and collapsed onto the couch beside me.

"How was he?"

"He was fine. Really. How are you?"

I was mortified when Cassandra threw her hands over her face and she began to weep. She was trying not to make any sound that would wake the baby, but her entire body shuddered in the attempt. I leapt to my feet and hurried to the vanity for a tissue. Cassandra took it from me without looking up.

"I miss Wesley's father," she whispered into her hands.

There was nothing I could say that would make her feel any better. "I'm sorry," was all I could offer, knowing it wasn't enough.

She took some time to collect herself. Then she said, "His name was Grant. He was the gardener."

"Here? At Willow Glen?" I had never surmised that much.

Cassandra nodded. "I used to watch him work sometimes, standing at my window in the mornings as I brushed my hair. He noticed me one day. After that he would look for me there and wave. He would give me the biggest, goofiest smile. He always looked so...*innocent.* Pure." The tears were drying on her face, and a warmth had begun to creep around the edges of her voice as she spoke of her lover.

"Eventually just a wave from him once a day wasn't enough. I began to take my meals out on the terrace during the daytime. He would take a break to climb the steps and said hello. I wouldn't call myself a timid person, but in the beginning I was very shy around Grant. He would try to draw me into conversation, but he seemed just as nervous, and at that point we could only find the most inane topics to discuss. Comments on the weather, that sort of thing. Usually I had butterflies in my stomach and couldn't eat much, so I would offer him some of my food, and he always cleaned my plate. Later I would joke that he was only interested in me for my food." She wrapped her arms around her shoulders. "The more time we spent together, the less shy we became with each other. You can probably imagine how things progressed from there. I warned him it wasn't the best idea, gave a vague explanation of my family not approving if they were to find out. But of course things like that never matter when it comes to love. Our time together seemed enchanted, it didn't seem possible that anything could alter what was happening between us. It seemed fated. For a while, life was pure bliss.

"But then I discovered I was pregnant. I told Grant we would be in great trouble when my family found out, but still I didn't think it necessary to tell him about the prophecy. In hindsight I realize that I should have, so that he would know exactly what we were up against. I tried to convince him to go, offered to help him escape. He wouldn't leave me. I was terrified for him, for us, and we clung to each other with the urgency of those who know their days together are numbered.

"My pregnancy wasn't showing yet, and I thought I still had time to convince Grant to run. I never guessed what he planned on doing. The poor, stupid brave man approached my father and declared his feelings for me. He told him he loved me, claimed our differences didn't matter, vowed to take care of me and the child. He didn't realize that his actions could mean death for us all."

I waited expectantly, but Cassandra didn't resume speaking. "And then what?" I prompted.

"And I never saw him again."

I was staggered. I don't know why I should have been, but I was. "What, just like that? What happened to him?"

Cassandra shook her head. "I don't know. A few days later the new gardener showed up and set to work."

Apparently the threats the Dorns made against humans weren't as empty as I could have hoped. The man loved by one of their own, just disappearing like that? A bitter acid taste worked its way up my throat as I thought about the fact that, if Victor had his way, that could be my fate as well.

"Did you never ask about him?"

"Of course I did. I ranted and raved, demanded to know what they had done with him. Mostly I was ignored. Jameson was the one who told me that Grant himself had approached our father about the whole thing. I know he would tell me more if he could. I'm sure the others wrung an oath from him to not say anything to me about what was done with Grant. In my more desperate moments I played on his guilt. I know I made him feel absolutely dreadful for not telling me." Cassandra clapped a hand over her eyes and the trembling of her shoulders grew more violent. Once she had managed to compose herself to a degree, she unfolded from the sofa and padded over to the vanity in her room, being careful to not wake the baby as she passed him. I watched her lift the lid off of a jewelry box. She pulled out the drawstring bag, the one I had snatched from beneath the floorboards of the gardener's cottage, and brought it over to where I sat. "This is all I have left of him."

She pulled on the cord, upending the bag. A hunk of rock fell out into her hand. She flipped it over and I saw it wasn't just any rock. Like the crystal flower Jameson had given to me, this had been skillfully shaped. It looked to be made of two different types of stone: one a pinkish gray with streaks of white thought it, the other a dark slate. Each had been fashioned into the shape of a heart and then melded to one another. Colors swirled together where the two hearts fused in the center.

"I made this for Grant as a token of our love. It was supposed to be our hearts entwined. Inseparable." She let slip a laugh, harsh and abrupt. "Silly, I know. I may have been twice his age in years, but it was still young love. My first true love." She hefted the charm in her hand, then slipped it back into its bag, pulling the cord tight.

"I don't think it was silly, I think it's sweet," I murmured, affected by her story. I cleared my throat. "How is it you guys do that, anyway? The molding thing?"

"It's a form of transmutation. Certain minerals and ores we can reshape, manipulating the bonds between molecules. It's difficult to explain the how of it to someone..."

"Human," I said, finishing the thought for her. Cassandra lifted her eyes, their color all the more brilliant after being awash in tears, and lifted a corner of her mouth sadly at me. She shrugged.

I leaned back in my chair and sighed. "You're wrong, though," I told her. Her look turned to one of curiosity. "That's not all you have left of him. You have his son. A living person made out of the love you two had for each other."

I worried that my words might send her back to weeping. They didn't, though, and she reached her hand out to cover mine. "Thank you, Anna."

"You're welcome, Cassandra."

Her attention returned to the treasure in her hand as she stroked her thumb back and forth over the soft material of the bag. She continued that way for a while, entranced. I decided to leave her to it, and rose to leave.

"You won't be needed to watch Wesley during the council meeting tomorrow," Cassandra said to me before I walked away. "I told my father that attending this farce was enough. I won't be going to the meeting. They can tell everyone I'm having a temper tantrum or something."

"Okay," I said, then asked something I had been wondering about. "Will your father be at the meeting? Isn't he afraid the others will see how sick he is?"

"He plans on arriving long before anyone else, so that by the time the others join him he will have been able to sit and rest and compose himself. He will also be the last to leave. In the meantime, he is going to let Victor do most of the talking for him."

"Oh." I imagined Victor loved that idea.

"Why don't you go enjoy the rest of the party?" Cassandra suggested. "At worst, you may get asked by someone to take away their empty glass."

"Maybe," I conceded. For the second time I told her, "Cassandra, I'm really sorry."

"Me too," she said softly.

I left her alone with her grief.

I ended up taking Cassandra's advice. I had no real desire to attend the dancing in the ballroom full of superhuman strangers, but the twinkling garden looked even more enchanting than usual and was calling to me. I flitted down the grand staircase and into the great hall. The doors to the ballroom stood open and I caught a glimpse of the room beyond. Great swaths of gossamer fabric stretched across the ceiling, drooping down in the middle with their ends tacked up. Everything was some shade of a peacock's colors: indigo, green or gold. I saw a lot of feathers and crystals. I could hear the string quartet playing from somewhere out of my line of sight. A wave of voices raised in drifted through the doors. As impressed as I was, that room was full of people I was probably better off staying away from, and so I moved on for the kitchen and slipped through the back door.

The terrace was awash in light. A bar was setup at one end, with a servant dispensing the drinks. The music from the ballroom wafted out through open windows, and the air was filled with the hum of many voices. Most of the people in sight actually looked the part of the Sentient that my mind had conjured up. Masked as they were, sill they were poised, they were posh, and of course they were all beautiful. A few stood out to me as looking more laidback, more approachable than their comrades.

I thought it unlikely that I would be served a drink if the general assumption was that I was a servant on duty, and so I bypassed the bar and skipped down the steps into the garden. I wandered down that path I had tread many times, soaking up the invigorating sensations around me. Despite the fact that I wasn't even included in this party, the celebratory ambiance still managed to seep into my pores. I found myself really wishing I could have that drink. The muted sound of the music, the voices, laughter and lights made for a heady mix.

The feeling was short-lived. I spotted something that sunk my spirits in an instant. There, on one of the benches arrayed around the fountain, was Jameson. He too wore a mask over his eyes, but there was no mistaking him. He sat close with a pretty blonde. The woman's hair fell in ringlets around the feathery white mask that covered her face, her hand was draped over Jameson's knee. His arm lay across the back of the bench behind her and he was leaning in close to say something into her ear. A wide smile was spread across her face.

I stepped off the path a ways into the shadows and watched them for a time. Why was she smiling so much? She was starting to look stupid, her face stuck open with that big grin. She arched her neck back and her laughter rang across the garden.

I mentally shook myself. I had known that Jameson was supposed to flirt with one of the other Sentient; Genevieve Valois, I thought I remembered her being called. He was to keep her amused and distracted. I shouldn't have let it get to me. It did, though. My body heated with anger, a warmth spreading from the center and out. I felt angry with Jameson for flirting with another woman, but was also upset with myself for feeling that way.

Who really was Jameson to me, anyway? He was someone with whom I could share what we had to offer. That's how he had put it, once. He was sexy and funny, and I enjoyed the time I spent with him. Most of it, at least. He was not, however, someone I had even thought to imagine spending my life with. How could that ever work? Never was it implied, by either of us, that what we had was serious, or exclusive.

All the same, I'm just not the kind of girl who is comfortable with open relationships like that. That became eminently clear when I saw Jameson with that woman and felt a wrenching in my gut. Call me traditional, but I prefer the exclusive, with at least the chance of becoming serious. So what the hell was I doing with Jameson? I think we can agree the circumstances I was in were pretty crazy, and so my responses and actions weren't the norm, either.

Regardless of all the reasoning and explanations, my mood had soured. I determinedly stepped back onto the path and continued on, walking right past the couple without being noticed. I followed the trail where it split to the right at the fountain and kept walking.

Fewer people milled around this far from the house. I wanted to distance myself from the others as much as I could. I kept walking until, as I came up to the gazebo, I heard my name called out.

"Anna! In here!"

Bewildered, I turned back around and approached the gazebo. Curious but wary, I mounted the steps.

Reza lay sprawled out on one of the wooden benches that circled around the gazebo's interior. On another stretched a petite Asian woman. It was hard to tell in the relative darkness under the pitched roof, but if I had to guess I would have put her in her early thirties. Of course, she was probably much older. Both of their masks lay discarded on the seats next to them.

"Come sit with us," Reza said, although neither of them was exactly sitting. "Anna, this is Alice Chen. Alice, Anna."

"A human, huh?" the woman introduced as Alice said. "You must think we're disgusting."

"Um, why is that?" I asked as I lowered myself down to sit.

Alice's hand fluttered in the general direction of the party and the other Sentient. "All of this stupid frivolity. Here we are, a highly evolved race of super humans, squandering our knowledge and abilities in the construction of a world of trivial pleasures."

"Oh. Well..."

"Excuse my friend for her bitterness. I mean, it's valid and all, but she shouldn't take it out on you."

"I just want to know what she thinks of us!" Alice griped.

"Of us, or of them?" Reza said, sitting up and gesturing over his shoulder. He planted his forearms on the tops of his thighs and clasped his hands together, fingers intertwined. He was wearing black dress slacks and a white button-down shirt that had been pulled untucked. A black tie hung loose around his neck. "Many Sentient have either forgotten or willfully abandoned the original intent of our forefathers. Do you know anything about esoteric alchemy?" he asked me.

"Can't say that I know much."

Alice swung herself upright into a sitting position as well. "No one knows about alchemy anymore, except what the stories propagate about the philosopher's stone or the elixir of life. A few well-read people might know about the contributions to gunpowder, cosmetics, metallurgy and liquor. Purely the corporeal stuff."

Reza looked me in the eye, a charged intensity writ in his face, like it was crucial that I understand what he wanted to tell me. "There's more to it than that. There's the physical aspects, sure, but they also serve as a sort of metaphor for the *spiritual*. Do you believe everyone has a soul, Anna?"

When I had stepped out into the nighttime revelry, I hadn't been prepared for any philosophical discussions. I answered as truthfully as I could. "I really don't know. I mean...no. I guess I don't. At least, not as some sort of ghost that keeps floating around after we die, or flies up into the clouds."

The answer seemed to satisfy Reza. He pursed his lips and nodded. "The ultimate goal was supposed to be personal transformation as part of a process of purification. Perfecting yourself, and not just in a cosmetic sense. I mean, it's not even necessarily religious, unless that's how you roll. It doesn't have to have anything to do with a god. It's just kind of like...no matter what you think happens to our essence when we die, whether our souls go to an afterlife or our energy gets reabsorbed into the world, you want to make sure what gets accepted back into the fold of the universe is something worth giving back. That's what I believe, at least."

"And here we are, many of our researchers stuck on searching for ways to keep ourselves looking hot, or achieving a totally amazing high," Alice scoffed.

"Well, not all of it's bad," Reza allowed, grinning.

Alice swung at him playfully. "But it's not the *point,*" she argued. Reza threw his hands up to fend off her blows.

Their sentiment was sounding familiar to me. "You know, I don't think you're the only ones who feel that way about it all," I told them.

"Yeah," Alice pulled a wry face, "but is anyone else willing to *do* anything about it?"

"Maybe this isn't the time or place to be talking about these things," Reza said, his voice dropping. "Let's lighten up, ladies. Get our chill on." Locking his hands behind his head, Reza lowered himself until he was once again lying down. Alice released an exasperated sigh, then flung herself down as well.

I rested against the back of my wooden seat and tried to take Reza's advice. The banter with my new companions had relaxed me. I found I was able to let the anger I had been carrying go, at least for the time being. I wanted to get the other feeling back. The anticipation of a party and what would come of it, the exhilaration of being outdoors at nighttime when the world was more mysterious and everyone's place in it less certain. I wanted the confidence that came when you were surrounded by people your instincts told you could be trusted. People whose perception of you and your purpose was so assured that you felt safer, more secure in yourself.

While these reflections swirled through my brain, Reza and Alice's volley's provided a comforting backdrop. I could almost believe this was a night like any other, hanging out with friends and not having a care in the world.

A sudden hush fell over the festivities. One after another, the white globes lighting up the garden winked out, and the lamps on the terrace, too. The color-changing fountain was the only remaining source of light. I looked to the others, perplexed.

"Ah," Reza said, "the light show is about to start."

I didn't notice anything at first, until a subtle glow began to radiate around us and finally I saw where it was coming from. What looked to be butterfly shapes made of light, of all different colors, were floating down from the sky around us. Each left a trail of light in its wake as it flitted by, a sparkling tail that faded gradually as the butterfly danced away. There were brilliant reds, blues, greens, bright yellows. As they glided into an object, such as a shrub or statue, they would burst in a halo of dazzling color and then fizzle out.

"Butterflies this time," Alice remarked. She craned her neck to look in my direction. "The light shows are Shahani's greatest contribution to our field. Viva la Sentient!" She yelled this last part, earning a halfhearted hushing from Reza.

"Cool it, Alice," he said over the sounds of her cackling. "Get control of yourself, sister."

I bit my lip, deciding if I dare disagree with them or not. It was obvious, though, that these two were nothing like Victor. I knew in my gut that I had nothing to fear from them. "You guys might condemn me for saying this, but I think it's absolutely beautiful."

Reza rolled his head to the side so that our eyes met again. "Of course it's beautiful. There are a lot of beautiful things in this world. And there's nothing wrong with enjoying them, but when it comes down to it, it's the essence of a thing that determines its value. What you find at the heart decides whether or not something is worthwhile. You know?" It sounded like a rhetorical question, but he looked at me so attentively, it was as if he was really waiting for my answer.

Alice cut in before I could think how to respond, reiterating, "Besides, that's *not the point*!"

A bright blue butterfly light flew into one of the posts on the gazebo and shattered into a cloud of color, raining down to the ground. I was feeling giddy all of a sudden. "I think Alice might benefit from that totally amazing high right about now," I said, not sure how my joke would be received. But Reza let loose one of his infectious laughs, and even Alice sniggered.

Reza extended both arms, showing empty palms. "Sorry, I'm fresh out these days. You know, the whole soul purification thing."

"Hey, some people say they're closest to enlightenment that way. In fact, I think I recall *you* used to make that argument," Alice said.

"Maybe I did," Reza admitted, a smile in his voice. "Time changes a man."

"Reza, you never change."

The butterflies had all dissolved by then and the globes hanging in the leaves flared back to life.

"Hey," Alice said, sitting up and shoving one of Reza's legs off of the bench. "Let's go walk or something. I need to burn off some of this energy." She leapt up from her seat and waved for me to follow as she skipped down the steps of the gazebo. I met Reza's eyes. He shrugged, and we got up to chase after her.

Heading in the opposite direction of the house brought us around a bend in the path that led to the koi pond. Here, too, were more globes of light. These rested atop lily pads, which glided over the water's surface in a serene dance, graceful and fluid. Now I really wondered what the trick was. Even if those were some sort of LED or battery powered lights, how was it possible for them not to sink, lodging in the muck at the bottom of the pond? Whatever those spheres were made of, glass or something else, they had to be too heavy to be borne so effortlessly.

I realized I didn't need to fear seeming too inquisitive around my companions. "How do those lights work?" I said, pointing.

Reza stepped to the bank of the pond near where one of the lily pads had drifted to the water's edge and squatted, scooping the orb up into cupped hands. He pivoted on his heels, extending his arms toward me so that I might get a better look. The light hovered, quivering slightly in the air just above his palms.

"You know that everything in this world is just energy in one form or another, right? Never comes from nothing, never just goes away. It's just a matter of converting it," he explained. I stared, entranced, as the orb's glow flared and faded erratically, mimicking a candle's flame. "Through alchemy we've just learned different ways to convert energy in the atmosphere around us into other things. We could probably manage to do amazing things with that power. But mostly we just make pretty sparklies." With this last, his tone lacked the irony I might have heard in a more bitter person's voice. After allowing me a moment to stare in awe, he lowered the light back into place. He nudged the lily pad back out toward the center of the pond and stood.

Alice plucked a stone from the ground and lobbed it at the water with a *plunk*. The nearest lily pads spun away toward the edges of the pond, riding the crests of the ripples she had made.

"What did those fish in there ever do to you?" Reza wanted to know.

"Oh, Reza. For a second I forgot about your bleeding heart. They were probably bored out of their little fishy skulls, anyway. I provided them with some excitement, that's all."

Amidst the banter, I felt something steal over me, making my fingers tingle. I felt...*playful.*

"You know, there's something I've been wondering about the Sentient," I remarked. Two pairs of questioning eyes turned my way. I stepped closer to the others. "So you guys can do all these super special nifty things, right? But what I really want to know is…can you float?" On the last word, I lunged forward with my arms outstretched and shoved at both Alice and Reza. With a yelp, Alice tipped over into the pond with a tremendous splash, limbs flailing. Reza lost his balance, wobbled, but regained his footing before falling into the water. He looked back at me with an answering mischievous glint in his eyes. I tried to spin away to run, but before I had even taken two steps, Reza wrapped his arms around me in a solid embrace and jumped, launching us both into the water.

For a moment the world became a landscape of swirling darkness, the water pressing in all around me. My head broke the surface, and I wiped at my eyes, snorting and laughing. I heard Reza's infectious laugh a few yards off to the side. I twirled around and saw Alice nearby, treading water. She blinked water out of her eyes before saying, "Well that was-"

"Frivolous?" I suggested.

"It's disgusting, really," Reza joined in the kidding.

Alice pursed her lips. "I was going to say unexpected. Like this." To emphasize these last words, she slapped her hands at the water, sending a spray at Reza. He spluttered and wiped at his face with his forearm, beads of pond water dripping from the ends of his hair.

"Oh, now it's on," Reza declared, and the three of us proceeded to have a battle of splashing. The sound of sloshing water was punctuated every now and again with our cries of indignation, and laughter.

This went on for the better part of fifteen minutes before I remembered myself, remembered where I was and *who* I was. I tried to sober up, regain some self-control and equanimity, but the grin wouldn't leave my face. I jerked my head toward the other Sentient milling about closer to the house.

"They must think we're nuts."

Alice paddled over to the pond's edge. "Nah, they've learned to expect this kind of nonsense from me and Reza," she said as she hauled herself out of the water. "They'll just ignore us and pretend they never witnessed such childish antics amongst their own."

I still had my doubts. "Maybe that's true for you guys, but I'm pretty sure I will have royally pissed off at least one or two people I can think of."

Reza had swum up behind me. He clapped a hand on my shoulder with a squelching noise. "We'll explain that it was all thanks to our bad influence on you. They'll believe it. Just tell us who."

"Appreciate it," I replied, pulling my own drenched body out of the pond. "But I hope it doesn't come to that."

We stood looking at one another for a minute, shedding water in puddles at our feet. Alice wrung out the hem of her shirt. Every now and again a clipped laugh would burst from one of us.

Eventually, my feeling of giddiness began to drain away along with the water dripping from my body. The truth about just how much trouble I might have gotten myself into hit home. Taking a dip in the ornamental pond certainly did not fit with my assumed role as a household servant. "Okay," I said, cutting into the atmosphere of revelry. "Seriously now, how are we supposed to get back to the house to change without drawing attention to ourselves?"

The others must have sensed the tightness that had clamped onto my voice. Their faces straightened. "We can always pretend you had no choice, that we were using you as a human plaything. Just try to look miffed, and put upon," Alice suggested.

I just couldn't shake the feeling that, with my luck, I would run straight bang into a supremely vexed Victor Dorn. I saw no other option, though, and so I agreed. "Alright. For what it's worth, I'm glad you guys called me over to hang out tonight. Even if the two of you are pretty frivolous and disgusting."

"I guess you're not so bad yourself, for a mere mortal," Alice countered.

"Good night, Anna," Reza said, his tone restrained. I saw worry for me reflected in his face. I tried to give him one last quick smile, to reassure him. That was my impression of Reza in the short time I knew him: he was always so concerned about the welfare of everyone else, and it made you let go of whatever was bothering you so that you could see him happy. You *wanted* to see him that way. As an added bonus, Reza's happiness had a way of seeping into everyone around him.

I turned away and began to march for the house, doing my best to look angry and annoyed in addition to soaking wet. Reza and Alice walked together a few yards behind, making a show of joking and laughing with one another.

I did notice several of the Sentient cast bewildered or disgusted looks our way, but I never saw Victor, much to my relief.

However, I couldn't help but also take note that, amongst the partygoers in the garden and in the house along the way to my bedroom, Jameson and the blonde woman were nowhere to be seen. The two of them had disappeared, somewhere away from everybody else.

10

August 1st, 2013

Once a favorite place to spend my time at Willow Glen, the garden mostly just makes me sad these days. Seeing it in its neglected state, the plants beginning to grow beyond their stations, overreaching themselves, drags my spirits down every time. I suppose I could try to do the work myself, spruce the place up a bit. But what would be the point?

I can't help but think of other times, past experiences I have had amid those leaves and blossoms, the waters and edifices of the Willow Glen garden. I feel discouraged. And then I get angry with myself. Angry for allowing myself to fall as far as I have, to be reduced to nothing better than a leaf being buffeted around by any wind that blew my way.

A good person once tried to help me see that I can take control over my own fortune, if I want to. I don't know that I was ready to hear him then. I still don't think I'm quite there. But I'd like to think that someday, and someday soon, I will be. I'll be ready.

The next day my whole body thrummed with anticipation. It had no right to, the events that were to take place had nothing to do with me. It's not as if I had been extended an invitation to the council meeting of the inscrutable Sentient. But my body didn't know any better, and trying to keep still felt like a million pins being driven into my flesh all over. Anytime I tried to sit I would leap back up seconds later, needing to move.

I knocked at Cassandra's door that morning, to ensure that she hadn't changed her mind about attending the meeting. She remained resolute and would be staying in her room with Wesley. I was not needed.

I stepped out into the garden. I wandered aimlessly for a short time before it dawned on me that I was hoping to chance upon someone, anyone. Finding the grounds empty, I turned for the house.

I tried to read a novel I had taken from the library, pacing my bedroom with the book held in front of my face, but my eyes kept scanning the same lines over and over without registering a single word.

I attempted yoga for a while, but somehow moving through the poses only made me feel more restless.

Matters changed abruptly when I decided to stop into the kitchen to see if Deborah needed any help. The housekeeper was not there. Instead a man who apparently was a servant from another household stood there, a tray balanced in each hand and a third sitting on the countertop next to him. The trays bore the assorted trappings for making tea: mugs, steaming pitchers of hot water, tea bags, and the like.

"Finally!" the man exclaimed, the irritated ruddiness on his face extending over a bald pate. "I've been waiting for someone else to show up to help me carry these. They called for tea nearly ten minutes ago! Here, take this one." Leaving me no time to argue, the man deposited a tray of mugs and saucers into my arms. He kept the other tray, slid his free arm under the third one and lifted it. He bustled right past me, calling back, "This way, swiftly now!"

I hesitated only a brief instant. Trying to pass myself off as just another human servant had apparently worked a little too well. On the other hand, it occurred to me that this man was expecting me to follow him to the council meeting itself, so that its members could be served their tea. A rush of exhilaration surged through me at the idea, and I hurried after him.

I have never worked as a waitress, and I was aware that I was trembling slightly at the thought of making an unsanctioned appearance at a gathering of the Sentient elite. I focused all my attention on not tipping my tray and sending the dishes crashing down to the floor.

We traversed the corridors, crossed the great hall, and stepped through the door to the library. One quick glance around the room showed that it was vacant. My confusion only lasted a moment before I saw that the secret door amidst the bookshelves stood wide open. The servant was making right for it.

Excitement and apprehension coursed through my body in equal measures when I realized I was gaining access to a place I had been told was off limits. It was too late to worry about the consequences, and I followed the eager servant through the yawning passage and into the room beyond. As I had been able to glimpse before, wooden bookshelves were arranged in rows within this inner-library. The books adorning them appeared aged. They were of all different sizes, spines of various heights jutting out with no regard for uniformity. Many were bound with either leather or what looked like vellum stretched over boards. Some had straps or tarnished clasps securing their covers shut.

Like the walls, the floor was stone-interlocking slabs of slate-and it was there I kept my eyes trained as I trailed behind the servant. As we advanced the pattern of the flooring differed in one spot and my eyes flitted over to see a mosaic of tiles, circular in shape and depicting some sort of design that I did not have enough time to study closely. I did note that in the center of the mosaic rose the pedestal I had spotted when Jameson had offered me a look into the room before, the one that bore an immense open tome. We hastened by the pedestal and all of the shelves and came to the other side of the room, where a large round table held court. Lined around the great table were members of the Sentient families that sat on the council, and I dared not look up for fear of meeting the disapproving eye of a Dorn.

The servant I had been following halted and spun on his heel, causing me to almost lose hold of my tray as I tried to pull up short to avoid smacking into him. He looked as terrified as I felt before we realized the crisis had been averted. Clamping his mouth shut tightly in annoyance, he indicated with his hand that I should go stand against the wall, where some of the other servants waited on hand in case they were needed. About a dozen people awaiting the council's pleasure. Heart hammering, I stepped away and took my place among them.

One of the others came to take the tray from me. My hands ached after I released my burden, from gripping it so tightly. I flexed stiff fingers and tucked my hands behind my back in imitation of the servants arranged next to me along the wall. The woman who had taken my tray hadn't moved. I glanced up and saw that it was none other than Deborah. She seemed dismayed to see me there, giving me a look that appeared both anxious and regretful. She leveled her eyes at me and gave an almost imperceptible shake of her head. She needn't have worried, the last thing I wanted to do right then was draw attention to myself and the fact that I was not supposed to be there.

I kept my face turned down, lifting my eyes from time to time to take in what was going on around me. Deborah and the servant I had found in the kitchen made their way around the table, serving the tea to those who indicated they wanted some, by either nodding their head or raising fingers at the servants' approach. I wasn't sure when exactly the meeting had started, but it must have been a couple of hours into it by then.

A stocky man whose white beard showed starkly against his dark skin was standing in front of his seat and speaking at length in a thick accent. I caught some of his words, something about distilling the unconscious and extracting truth, but as his voice droned in my ears I was more interested in stealing peeks at the room and its occupants. From my location I had a side-view of Nathaniel, leaning forward onto arms propped on the tabletop. I wondered if anyone else noticed how gray he looked. How could they not? On his one side sat Victor and Zahira, mostly their backs turned my way. On his other side was Jameson.

I scanned the rest of the people seated at the table, recognizing a few from the night before and from encountering them around Willow Glen and its grounds as they arrived. At the far side of the table from where I stood sat Reza, although "lounged" might be a more fitting word for how he had arranged himself, leaning back with elbows hanging over the arms of his chair, his hands clasped in front of his stomach. To his right were two men I took to be his brother and father. The men looked very similar, one a younger version of the other. Their hair was much tamer than the youngest Hakim's; straight, black and flat against their heads. On Reza's other side sat a woman who was presumably his mother. Her long black hair, parted in the center, spilled down over her arms. She sat perfectly straight, hands folded on the table before her.

The room was bathed in a golden glow. I snuck a look up and saw more of those light globes nested in sconces along the walls, shining with a yellow radiance. Banners displaying various coats of arms were hung high up around the room, perhaps a couple dozen of them. I wondered which one represented House Dorn.

My gaze slid off the walls and froze when I found myself looking directly into Jameson's eyes. He raised his eyebrows at me. I saw his lips twitch, but whether it was in amusement or annoyance I couldn't decipher. He returned his attention to the man who had been speaking, whose oration seemed to be winding down.

As the man made his concluding remarks, it was Victor, standing in for Nathaniel in leading the proceedings as head of the hosting family, who addressed him and the rest of the congregation. "Fascinating subject matter, Khem. I'm certain I speak for all of us when I say I look forward to hearing of your findings as you probe further into this domain." Victor clapped his hands together. "Now, I believe Khem was the last one with a prepared presentation. If there are no further questions for him, does anyone have any other topics or concerns they would like to bring up at this time?"

"I do," spoke the woman sitting next to Reza.

"Nimra, yes," Victor answered, holding out his hands in a gesture for her to speak her mind.

The woman unfolded her hands, placing them side by side on the tabletop. "Esteemed colleagues, I feel impelled to bring up a matter we have come up against these past many years. The men and women who first delved into the arts of alchemy set our kind on a fine path, with noble purpose. But they were men and women like any other, and they were constrained within the circumstances of their lives, in a specific time and place. Many of the prescriptions they left for their successors, namely us present here, were well-intended and meaningful when they were devised. However," she swept smoldering eyes around to each of the others at the table. "Times have changed. Regulations that were appropriate when they were first conceived may no longer be so. As times and circumstances have changed, so must we Sentient. And this includes taking a hard calculating look at some of our inherited policies."

I was reminded of what Cassandra had once divulged, about her own mother and this Nimra Hakim discussing the need to do away with the power of each family being inherited by the eldest child rather than the one who was most qualified.

"Such as?" a refined woman with her gray hair twisted up into a sleek chignon wanted to know. She sat two spaces away from Jameson. It was then I noticed that sitting in between them, directly to Jameson's right, was the blonde woman, the one I had seen him with the night before. Genevieve. She sat leaning to the side in her chair, her arm nearly touching Jameson's. Perhaps it *was* touching.

A silence stretched through the room, until a man who looked to be part of Alice's family spoke up. "There is the ruling to have any Sentient who spawns a half-breed child killed, along with the infant."

The reaction was immediate. The Dorns all snapped their heads in the man's direction, and several voices began calling out at once.

"I've felt that one should have been done away with for decades," I heard someone say. A woman asked, "Why change what has worked up to this point?" and someone responded, "It has never worked! That decree in particular is brutal and archaic." Another voice cried, "Leave ourselves open to being undermined? You do recall the prophecy, don't you?"

"Funny thing about prophecies," Reza's even voice rang through the clamor. "If they're true, then they will come to pass no matter what you do."

Murmuring ensued all around the table as neighbors discussed the matter, some of them more animatedly than others. The Dorns remained silent, watching with keen interest to see how things played out. Several minutes passed in this manner, the air in the great space agitating with the mass of voices. Finally Nathaniel raised a hand. Gradually the others took notice and the din began to die down.

Once the room fell quiet, Nathaniel eased himself up to standing, pressing his hands against the table for support. I had to strain to hear his words. "I must say I rather agree with Nimra on this subject. There are many such provisions that have become outdated, have outgrown their suitability. I propose we do away with this one affair, the killing of Sentient parent and half-breed child. Let us vote here and now."

"Altering the word of the originators," one man said. "Is this not sedition?"

"It is mercy," Nathaniel answered.

Victor slammed a fist onto the table, making me flinch. He leapt from his chair, knocking it backwards to the floor. "It is *weakness*!" he declared.

All eyes turned to Victor. "Dare we question the wisdom of our forebears?" he spat.

"Yes," a female voice uttered. I think it might have been Alice.

Victor glared all around the table, but when he failed to identify the culprit he ignored the remark and went on as if no one had spoken. "I say to do so is spineless! I say some of those among us have their priorities misaligned! Those who are supposed to lead our prestigious line on the path laid out by the first men to recognize our true destiny. Those who-"

"ENOUGH!" Nathaniel bellowed with more force than I would have believed he could possibly wield in his state. Indeed, as soon as the word was out he fell into a fit of coughing. Everyone watched in stunned silence as his whole body shook with the strength of the hacking that overcame him. He held an arm in front of his mouth. It seemed the bout would never end.

Finally the coughing lessened. Nathaniel stood bent over and as he pulled his arm away from his face there were splotches of blood on his sleeve. Someone gasped.

Jameson stood from his own chair. "Ladies and gentlemen," he intoned in a sober voice, "I pronounce this council meeting concluded. *Scire est mutare.*"

"*Scire est mutare,*" the others recited back, their voices small and uncertain.

Victor spun around and stormed away. Zahira scrabbled out of her own chair and hurried out of the room after him. Jameson grasped his father's arm and guided him back down into his seat. Unsure, the others began standing. A person here and there, and soon the rest. They filed out of the room, making a point of not staring at Nathaniel as they passed.

The taint of unease spilled over to the servants as well; none seemed sure if and when they were supposed to follow the others out. Only Nathaniel and Jameson remained. The blonde woman stalled until Jameson motioned with his head that she should leave as well. One by one the servants peeled away from the wall and made for the door.

I jogged over to the table. Reaching for Nathaniel's wrist I felt for his pulse. It was weak and the rhythm was irregular.

"I fear," Nathaniel puffed, "I shall...pass out." Seconds later he lost consciousness, drooping in his chair. Jameson threaded his arms around his father's body to support his weight. I kept my fingers over his pulse to make certain it wasn't getting any worse, watched the steady rise and fall of his chest. The man had been running on fumes to begin with. Exerting himself as he had took all of his reserves, but his faint would probably be self-limiting while his body recuperated. He would wake on his own in a matter of time.

Jameson looked at me over his father's lolling head. "Do you think the two of us could get him to his room?"

I wanted to be able to say yes, but I doubted I possessed the physical strength to help carry the deadweight of an adult man. I shook my head. "I don't think so. Let me find someone else to help."

"I don't want anyone else seeing him this way," Jameson argued.

"Maybe I can find Frederick?"

He looked at me, his eyes boring into me as they usually did, then nodded tersely. "Fine. Hurry." I turned on my heel and dashed out of the room.

There was no one in the outer-library. The great hall, on the other hand, was in chaos. The other Sentient had amassed there and were in the throes of deep conversation. They huddled in groups, talking quietly. I scanned the crowds for Frederick. There was no sign of him. Trying to remain as inconspicuous as possible, I lowered my head and cut through the crowd, walking swiftly in the direction of the kitchen.

Just as the Sentient were gossiping in the great hall, so were the servants in the kitchen. I spotted Deborah with little trouble and came up to her side. "Deborah-" She turned toward me, her face gray and strained. She clapped her hands over her cheeks. "Have you seen Frederick?" I asked.

Deborah swung her head from side to side. "No, dear. I haven't the faintest where Frederick is at the moment. He wasn't one who was assigned to attend at the meeting." She shook her head, still clamped between her palms. "Oh, this is simply terrible! The poor master!"

I gripped the housekeeper's shoulder in a gesture I hoped came across as comforting before hurrying away on my hunt for the butler.

Back in the great hall, I glanced up the stairs and despaired at how large of an area I had to search through. Before I could muster the energy to take a step toward the staircase, I heard my name called from somewhere behind me. Turning around I saw Reza and Alice leaning against the wall. When he caught sight of my face, Reza pushed himself upright and looked at me with worry. "Anna. What is it?"

I tried to think quickly. Just how angry would Jameson be with me...? In the end I made the decision that felt right to me and stepped over to join Reza and Alice. I filled them in on the situation and pleaded for their help. "And even if we carry him out, we can't bring him through here with everybody hanging around." They looked at one another. Reza nodded, and Alice strode toward the center of the room and clapped her hands over her head.

"Listen up, everybody!" she shouted. "I think we could all use some fresh air. Let's move this party out to the terrace, shall we? Come on, let's go. Look lively, now."

Some of the others exchanged confused looks, but Alice was insistent. She actually poked a finger into the sides of an indignant few, flitting away through the crowd before they could manage a rebuke. Gradually the throng began meandering toward the door in the back.

"Let's go," Reza said softly, and I followed him back to the library.

As we approached I could see the muscles of Jameson's jaw twitch and he gave me a hard look. "You seem to have forgotten what the butler looks like."

I threw my hands into the air. "I couldn't find Frederick, and I didn't think you wanted to wait while I ran all over Willow Glen looking for him. Reza will help us."

Jameson took a deep breath and let it out slowly. He blinked a few times, clearing the irritation away. He looked to Reza appraisingly.

"I got this," Reza assured him.

I stood back and watched as the two of them lifted Nathaniel between them and shuffled for the door. I trailed behind them, lingering when I came up to the pedestal on the tiles. I would have loved to have taken the time to get a closer look at the pages of the great book it held, but I knew I had a duty elsewhere. Regardless of my own circumstances, Nathaniel was my patient. Though I was confident he would pull through that particular episode once he had time to recover, my place was by his side, providing whatever small measures of comfort I could. I pulled myself away from the tempting wealth of information before me and hurried to his chambers.

When I reached Nathaniel's rooms, Jameson and Reza were lowering his limp frame onto his bed.

"That will be all," Jameson was quick to inform Reza, "thank you." Reza turned, dipped his head in my direction, and left. I set to removing the unconscious man's shoes and trying to arrange him more comfortably in the bed. Even as I did so, his eyelids began to flutter.

"Father?" Jameson said gently. Nathaniel's eyes opened all the way and found his son's face. He kept them there for several seconds, then let them slip closed again and emitted a drawn out sigh. "Father, do you recall what happened?"

More seconds passed before Nathaniel answered, not bothering to open his eyes again. "Sorry to say, I do."

I motioned for Jameson to help me lift his father's shoulders so that I could slide another pillow beneath him. "I'll have Deborah bring you up some orange juice or something," I told him. "A little sugar might help. What else can I do for you, Nathaniel?" I searched for something helpful to say, something comforting. *"Sorry your son is such an asshole"* seemed sadly inadequate.

"Please," the broken man muttered, "I wish to be alone for a time."

Jameson looked like he wanted to argue, but held his tongue. We left Nathaniel to himself, but brought our apprehensions with us as we stepped out of his chambers together. We spent a long minute standing motionless in the hallway, uncertain of how to proceed. Jameson rubbed a rough hand over his face and finally made to move. "Come," he said, "let's fill in my sister."

We walked without speaking. Jameson, who usually looked so put together, had dark circles under his eyes, and I couldn't help but wonder if something blonde and giggly had kept him up late the night before. A voice of reason piped up in my head, chiding the other, arguing that the man was dealing with the decline of his one remaining parent. Besides, so what if he had spent the night with another woman? I wasn't fond of that idea, sure, but if I was being honest with myself the man was more captor to me than he was a boyfriend.

Still, the thought turned my stomach. I wanted to understand exactly what was going on, preferred to know all the details of the huge mess I was in, even if I found them less than appealing. Of course, that would apply to most of them. I wished I knew what was going through Jameson's head, what he thought it was we had; but it was clearly not an appropriate time to hold that discussion. I clenched my teeth and kept that conversation for another time.

Cassandra was standing in the middle of her room when we arrived, holding Wesley to her shoulder and swaying. "What's wrong?" she asked as soon as she saw our faces.

Jameson told his sister about the council meeting, what Nimra Hakim had said and how the other Sentient had responded. "The very first thing someone brought up was the decree to end the lives of half-human children and the Sentient responsible for producing them." He grunted, a laugh without humor. "How narrow-minded of us to think we were the first Sentient family to ever find ourselves in this position! With how quickly heated that discussion became, I'm certain others have had personal cause to question that ruling before. I believe you are in good company, little sister."

"It seems I missed out on quite the pivotal council meeting. *Scire est mutare*," Cassandra remarked, her voice rife with irony.

"Those words," I said, "I recognize them. They're inscribed on the wall at the entrance to the estate, aren't they?"

"They are," Cassandra answered. "They mean 'to know is to change.'"

"It's the Sentient motto. Ra ra ra," Jameson added in a bleak voice.

"You'd make a horrendous cheerleader," I told him. I thought about those words, to know is to change. Of course in my case the change wasn't a physical one, but from the moment I passed through that gate and came to Willow Glen, I had learned a great many things I would never have even thought possible. Without a doubt I felt changed by the knowledge. Something at the very center of what made me who I was had shifted, something immutable, and I don't think there's any going back after something like that. If I ever got my own life back, I was going to have to redefine my 'normal'.

Jameson went on to describe the confrontation between their father and Victor, and the meeting's explosive finale when Nathaniel had coughed up blood in front of all the other Sentient. Cassandra's eyes widened as she listened.

"No! How did they react?"

"They are confused, and frightened. They are cowed for now, but once they leave Willow Glen in the morning and have more time to talk it over with one another, they will become braver and begin asking uncomfortable questions."

"Oh, poor Father," Cassandra breathed. Her lower lip began to tremble. "How humiliating, to be challenged like that in front of the entire council. And it's all my fault."

"Hush now," Jameson scoffed, wrapping an arm around his sister's slender shoulders, his hand coming to cradle the top of Wesley's head. He stroked the baby's silken hair with his thumb. "Of course this is not your fault. Victor has always been a right bastard, since long before you were born. This day was going to come eventually. It was inevitable." Cassandra sniffled and nodded, sweeping the tears from beneath her eyes. "We just have to keep everyone pretending everything is normal until the others all leave tomorrow. Then we'll figure out how to fix this. Let's just get through until tomorrow."

What all three of us left unspoken was the thought that even after we made it safely to the next day, Nathaniel's time seemed to be running out.

11

August 4th, 2013

I have come to a point in my story that makes me weary of writing. In fact, I haven't written at all over the past few days. I haven't done much of anything except feel sick and tired of it all.

Really, I barely even drag myself out of bed these days.

Sick. And tired.

But it needs to be told and there is no point in putting it off any longer. I might as well just take the plunge. And so here I go...

If I thought that I would be cured of my restlessness after everything that had happened at the council meeting, I was wrong. If anything it only worsened. Something of great significance had occurred, something that was sure to lead to trouble, and I couldn't bear to sit idly in my bedroom and not know what was going on. By evening I gave up trying and stole out of my room and down the stairs to see if I could discover anything, shed any more light on the fallout of that afternoon's course of events.

The place was all but abandoned. For a large house full of guests, all was eerily quiet. I took it as an ominous sign; surely under usual circumstances the Sentient would spend their last evening visiting with one another and engaging in different forms of entertainment?

The great hall was empty. I could hear a clamor from the kitchen, the sounds of dishes being cleaned up and food being put away. No voices, though. It seemed even the servants from the different households were too subdued to speak much.

I stuck my head just inside the doorways of the dining and drawing rooms, ascertaining that they, too, were vacant. It was only in the library that I sensed the first signs of other life. I did not see anybody, but could make out the sound of voices carried out from the inner sanctum through that passageway that yawned open still. I approached with light footsteps, not sure who I would see when I crossed that breach. It was with immense relief that I saw it was none other than Reza and Alice. I strode over to where they sat, just the two of them at the large council table.

"Am I glad to see you two. It's like a mausoleum here tonight."

"Generally mausoleums are much more peaceful than this place is right now, I think. Not nearly as much of an underlying sense of tension among the dead," Alice replied. Reza held a hand out to one of the other chairs at the table, offering me a seat.

"Yeah. Pretty crazy what happened today, huh?" I said, sitting down and shifting uneasily, hoping they wouldn't ask me to tell them more than I could share in good conscience.

"Oh, with Dorn? Yeah, that was pretty weird. Your friends here are going to have a lot to answer for, once everyone leaves here and grows a pair. Then they can challenge them to explain what the hell is going on from a safe distance."

Reza sat leaning forward in his own seat. He twisted at the waist to face me. "Even as far as things that were said at the council meeting before that, though. Alice and I have some concerns."

I tried to think back to the pieces I had overheard at the meeting before things had blown up at the end. I didn't have to wonder long, though, before Reza explained. "This 'dowsing' thing that Khem Massri was going on about. Being able to fish information out of other people's minds. Sure, maybe it sounds pretty sweet in theory, but in practice-"

Alice cut in, finishing Reza's thought for him. "It's unethical and downright diabolical. How will that help us better ourselves as a people?"

"We've forgotten our purpose, Anna," Reza continued, his voice dropping in pitch, somber. "Now it's all about control. Shaping the world to better suit us, and not the other way around."

Not for the first time since coming to Willow Glen, I felt the hairs on my arms stand on end with almost electric intensity. "Well," I said, tucking my hands under my legs. "Not all of you are like that."

"Yes, Reza and I are a couple of real roses among thorns," Alice retorted.

I shook my head. "It's not just you two. I think there are more than you realize who feel the same way you do." I saw their eyes meet, and hold. I had tried to tell them as much before, but now it seemed they gave the idea more serious consideration.

"I hope you're right," Reza murmured after a minute.

"On that note," Alice said, stretching her arms above her head, "the sooner we retire for the evening, the sooner it will be morning and we can leave this farce behind."

"Not sure it's that easy," Reza replied, "but my mother did ask me to stop in and have a word with her, so I probably shouldn't keep her waiting."

Reza and Alice stood from the seats, and a moment later I followed suit. I was sorry to lose the company so soon.

"Goodnight," Alice said with a wave of her hand.

Reza tipped his chin at me. "Anna."

"Goodnight, guys," I answered. I watched them walk away, a hollowness expanding inside of my chest. I had just about resigned myself to the fact that I had little choice but to withdraw to my own room and face the rest of the night alone. That was when I noticed it again, the pedestal with the book. I realized I had the perfect opportunity to study it up close.

I crossed over to the mosaic spread around the base of the display, almost fearing I would be struck down for blasphemy. The powers that be showed mercy and I reached my goal unscathed. The round shape the tiles formed actually encompassed several other concentric circles within its bounds, and a triangle at the very center. At regular intervals within each ring were different cryptic symbols. There was one that reminded me of a pitchfork on its side. Another began and ended with flat lines but formed an inverted arch in the middle. Some I would recognize in the pages of the book on the history of alchemy Jameson had handed to me my first night at Willow Glen: spirit, life, earth.

Burning with curiosity, I peered into the open book. Right away I understood it to be a book of genealogy. Closer inspection revealed that it was the Dorn family tree displayed on the page I was seeing. The names were written in a cramped, spidery script. I had to lean in close to decipher the letters. The last names recorded were Victor, Jameson and Cassandra. No Wesley, of course, and no trace of the human who had sired him.

I pinched the edge of the page gently between two fingers and lifted it to see what came on the following pages. There were more names, more family lineages. None that I recognized. I let the page drop back down in place. I realized my curiosity had soured at the glaring omissions from the Dorn family line. One could speculate that there hadn't been time yet to fill in the additional information, but of course I knew better. The names of Wesley and his father would never be added to that book. I stepped away and turned for the door.

My restlessness was as ardent as ever, but my options were limited and I decided there was nothing for it but the return to my room for the night. I hoped only that it passed quickly.

The next morning dawned pale and subdued, cloud cover muting any light the sun would have shone down on us. Everything felt distant. The visiting Sentient families were each taking their leave one by one after breakfast, but mentally it seemed they had already checked out. They were absorbed in their thoughts of all they had to tell those who hadn't been at the council meeting, or else perhaps they were still struggling with their own reactions to everything that had transpired. None tarried for long.

As for myself, I couldn't eat much that morning. I felt like there was a hole in my gut, but not one that could be filled by food. I loitered in the great hall, not wanting to miss the chance to say goodbye to Reza and Alice.

The Hakim family was one of the last to depart. A decidedly surly Victor was keeping a stiff post by the main doors to see everyone off. Every so often he would send an icy glare my way, making it clear he saw no need for me to be there.

Zahira stood by her husband's side bidding farewell to everyone as they left, her voice apologetic. While the rest of the Hakim family approached the two of them Reza made his way over to me, a bulging duffel bag slung over his shoulder.

"Hi," I said, then wondered what kind of way that was to start off making a goodbye.

"Hi," Reza answered with his crooked smile.

I hugged my arms to myself. I don't know why I suddenly felt so reserved with him. Maybe it was a manner of protection, an attempt to shield myself from the fact that he was the closest thing I had to a friend and ally, and now he was leaving and I was going to miss him. "So, thanks again. For everything."

"It's no problem," he responded. "I'm glad we had a chance to meet, Anna. If you ever find yourself in Marrakesh, be sure to look us up."

"I don't foresee my life taking me to Morocco anytime soon," I replied. I was trying to sound sarcastic, but I'm afraid I may have just sounded pathetic. Reza looked at me quizzically before replying.

"You know, Anna, life isn't something that always has to happen *to* you." He regarded me a moment longer, then offered a gentle smile. "You take care, okay?"

"I'll try. You too."

"I always do."

I watched as Reza rejoined his mother, father and brother. Zahira hugged each of her relatives in turn, Victor nodded at them woodenly, and then they were gone.

I waited for a while longer to see if I might catch Alice as she left, but the Chens must have gone before I took up my watch in the great hall and I never saw her. Before I gave up, however, I witnessed the departure of the Valois family. Genevieve approached Victor and her voice carried over to where I stood as she inquired as to whether Jameson was around to see them off as well.

"I don't know where he is," Victor answered, and did not elaborate.

Genevieve's shoulders slumped. "Oh. Well, could you please see this letter delivered to him for me, then?" She handed a small square envelope to Victor, who gave a brusque nod as he accepted it. Genevieve's regal-looking mother laid a hand on her daughter's shoulder and guided her out the door. The tall white-haired man with them who I took to be Genevieve's father hung back and stepped closer to Victor. His voice was elegant yet forceful, imperious in effect. He leaned in toward Victor, yet still his voice rang throughout the room.

"You must know everyone is in an uproar. It's clear that none of you wish to explain what happened with your father yesterday. But keep in mind that this does not only concern yourselves. Whatever is going on with Nathaniel could very well have consequences for us all. You must see that we require answers." Even from across the room I could see Victor turn gray, his face grow tight. Before he found his tongue, the other man clapped a hand on his shoulder. "It is plain that these are not the right circumstances for discussing this. See to your father. Confer with your family. But know the Council expects an explanation within one week's time." He nodded at Victor, who hardly looked comforted, and then left to catch up with his wife and daughter.

Scarcely waiting for the man to cross the threshold, Victor tossed the envelope he held onto a nearby side table up against the wall and began to massage his temples.

"Well, that should be the last of them, then," I heard Zahira say.

"Good. Now we can suffer the humiliation of our family in peace. For one more week, at least."

Zahira clucked her tongue. "Come, Victor. Let's go back to the children. They worry, not knowing the details about what happened yesterday, but sensing your distress."

"My distress, or the disgrace of their grandfather?"

Not deigning to answer, Zahira linked her arm through Victor's and led him away.

Finding myself alone in the great hall, I couldn't stop my eyes from zeroing in on where the envelope lay discarded on the side table. I knew the best thing to do would to just leave it be and put it from my mind. Instead I crossed the room and lifted it into my hands, disgusted with myself even as I did so. Flipping the envelope over, I saw that where the flap had been sealed was an impression of Genevieve's pursed lips marked in lipstick. I rolled my eyes and fought the urge to make a gagging noise. There was no one around, but sound carried in that cavernous space. I didn't want to have to explain to anyone what I was doing retching over a note addressed to someone else.

Tucking the envelope into my back pocket, I climbed the staircase and made for my bedroom. As I approached I saw that Jameson waited in the hall outside of my door, pacing with arms crossed in front of his chest. He halted when he caught sight of me and stood waiting. I slowed as I came closer.

"What, so now we're going to pretend you can't just let yourself into my room whenever you want to?" I challenged.

Jameson's eyes flitted over me, calculating. "Ah. I know that look. Someone is not very pleased with me. That's a look I happen to know all too well. I just wasn't expecting to see it from you."

I slipped the envelope out of my pocket and held it up so that he could see the lipstick.

"What's this?" he asked.

"It's a letter from your darling Genevieve," I responded.

"Ah yes, darling Genevieve. She wrote you a note, did she?" he inquired mockingly. When I refrained from answering he lifted his chin. "I see. It's a note addressed to me. Perhaps she asked you to deliver it for her? No? I didn't realize you were the thieving type."

"You don't really know anything about me, now do you?" I retorted. All at once my anger deflated, though, and I came to realize that maybe it had been an affectation all along. It's not like I was in love. I liked Jameson, he was fun and he was sexy, but was he really anything more than an entertaining distraction from my predicament, a method of escape? Would the two of us have ever hooked up if circumstances hadn't thrown us together the way they did? Maybe.

But maybe not.

I asked myself if I was truly upset, deep down where things really mattered. I didn't think I was. The answer caught me by surprise, but brought a measure of relief as well. I let the hand clasping the envelope fall to my side. "You know what?" I said. "It doesn't matter. Please forget any of that just happened."

I passed by him and inserted my key into the lock on my bedroom door. Pushing the door open I took a step into the room before I was stopped by Jameson's voice.

"Anna."

I turned back to face him.

"I would like my letter, please." From the taut set of his jaw I could tell I had angered him. I held the envelope out against his chest and when his hand rose up to grip it I patted him through the paper before shutting the door. I don't think he knew if he should interpret the gesture as derisive or conciliatory. Oddly enough, at that moment it didn't really much matter to me either way.

When I checked in on Nathaniel later he was dressed but in bed, sitting propped up by several pillows. I pulled back the covers to assess for swelling in his lower body. I can't say I was surprised to find his feet blown up to the point where the skin was stretched tight and cool to the touch. I probed around for his pulse, but there was too much fluid in the way.

His upper extremities didn't seem to be as swollen as the lower ones, and I wanted to feel for the pulse at his wrist. I noticed he had a necklace of some sort clutched in his hand, its silver chain dangling from his fist.

"What's that?" I asked.

Nathaniel unfurled his fingers, revealing a sizeable oval pendant adorned with a delicate filigree. He struggled with the clasp on its side before separating the halves of the pendant, pulling open what turned out to be a locket. I leaned in closer and saw that in one half was a minute black and white photograph of a man and woman, her hands on his shoulders and his arm around her waist. On the other side was a picture of three small ginger-haired children.

"Is this you guys?" I said, incredulous. "You and your wife? Cassandra, Jameson and Victor?"

"Mmm," Nathaniel replied in way of affirmation. "Vivienne was never without it. Wore it right up to her dying day." He snapped the locket shut, his fingers curling around it once more.

I touched two fingers softly to the hollow at the side of his wrist. The rush of his blood could be detected there, but it worried me how slowly his heart seemed to be pumping. I remembered the first time I examined him when his heart had been in overdrive. This was worse. But then, we knew he had been deteriorating.

"Nathaniel-"

"You need not say a thing, Miss Cassidy. I know." His body convulsed on the bed as he coughed. "Please, don't concern yourself too much. What will be, will be. However...I would appreciate your assistance getting down to dinner this evening, if you would be so kind."

I shook my head. "You still want to sit for dinner? You know you don't need to push yourself like that. I'm sure everyone will understand."

Nathaniel looked up and met my eye for the first time since I had entered his room. "I want it to be known that I'm still here, and I'm still in charge."

I couldn't argue with that, and so I put his socks back on and left Nathaniel as I had found him. At dinner time I helped him hobble down to the dining room.

All of the usual family members were present for dinner. They were all in the same room for the first time since the altercation at the council meeting. No one broached the subject, but I'm sure it was on everyone's mind. It was yet another meal filled for the most part with a tense quiet.

Nathaniel did not eat at all. He did, however, still have the locket clasped in his hand.

Victor noticed his father wasn't eating. He wouldn't deign to look at the man when he said, "You can't expect to get better if you don't eat."

"I should think, then, that you would be pleased I am not eating."

Victor's knife clanged against his plate. "Oh, come off it. Just because I don't agree with you on...*many* things, doesn't mean I want you dead. Now please stop being so melodramatic. You are not dying. You're just sick, for whatever damned reason, and you need to eat to keep up your strength."

I scanned Victor's face. Was he really that naive? Couldn't he *see* his father was dying? Or was he so blinded by the fact that their kind never usually died from illness that, despite not being able to deny his father's sickness, he still couldn't accept that it was going to spell his end?

I looked to Jameson, but he was glaring fixedly at the food on his plate, stabbing it mercilessly with his fork.

The conversation went no further. Nathaniel still did not eat.

After the rest of us had finished our meals, Victor stood and asked, "Shall we retire to the drawing room?"

Jameson thrust himself against the back of his chair. "Have we not put up with each other enough for one evening?" he asked, voice saturated with disgust.

"What this family needs, little brother, is to learn to get along. Divided, we will only be fodder for the other Sentient families."

"And where was this sentiment when you challenged and insulted our father in front of the most prominent members of the other Houses?" Jameson argued.

The veins in Victor's neck bulged as he choked back whatever it was he really wanted to say. "If you had any sense you would see that I am trying to make amends. Now please. To the drawing room."

I glanced around the table. One by one, the others began to rise and follow Victor. Nathaniel indicated that he wanted me to help him navigate his way there along with the rest. I wrapped an arm around one of his, feeling his clammy skin. Once we reached our destination I kept hold of his arm as he lowered himself into his chair, then took my own place on the sofa. Like so many nights before, Victor poured the brandies and passed them around, Evelyn placing one into her grandfather's free hand.

I had grown more appreciative of the liquor since my arrival at Willow Glen, and that night I was especially grateful as I swallowed it down and felt my senses burn. I saw Jameson wasted no time downing his own drink, either.

Since he had not eaten any dinner, I wasn't sure that Nathaniel would be partaking in the after-dinner drinks, but he did bring his tumbler to his mouth and take a small sip. Almost immediately he erupted into a fit of coughing. He smacked his glass down on the end table and raised his arm to cover his mouth. The others stared into their glasses, as if pretending not to notice the outburst while it went on would spare Nathaniel's feelings. But with time the coughing only seemed to get worse and no one could ignore it any longer. The force of his hacking escalated, his face turned purple. He leaned forward, trying to catch his breath between the spasms racking his body. The locket slipped out of his hand and fell to the floor in a heap.

"Let's get him down before he blacks out again," I said to Jameson.

"What do you mean 'again'?" Victor demanded. Jameson and I hurried to Nathaniel's side, neither one of us bothering to answer the question. Nathaniel was gasping for air. Just as we reached him his eyes rolled back and he slumped forward into our arms.

I met Jameson's eyes over the top of his father's head. "Is he...?" Jameson said, his words trailing off. The coughing had stopped but the rasping sound of Nathaniel laboring to breathe could still be heard.

"Let's just get him to his bed again," I answered.

"Victor," Jameson bit out, and the two men stood next to their father, one by each side, and braced his weight on their shoulders. They carried him away much like Jameson and Reza had done just the day before.

"Children, go to your rooms," Zahira instructed before following the men.

"But Mother, what's wrong with him?" Julian wanted to know, voice shrill with alarm.

"Shush, don't bother them," Evelyn told her brother, draping an arm over his shoulders and leading him from the room. I went after the others.

This time Nathaniel began to resurface from his stupor while still en route to his bedroom. From where I trailed behind I could hear him making weak sounds of protest at being carried along by his sons. His objections were ignored and the men finally settled him on top of his bed. Still his breathing sounded coarse.

"You're probably weakened because you didn't eat at dinner," Victor conjectured.

Nathaniel knew better. "The grandchildren," he whispered through dry lips. "I want to see my grandchildren."

Victor turned to his wife, one hand still clamped onto his father's shoulder. "Zahira, fetch Evelyn and Julian."

With a terse nod of her head Zahira spun toward the door, but the sound of Nathaniel's voice, this time with more force behind it, stopped her short.

"I wish to see *all* of my grandchildren."

"What do you-" Comprehension dawned and Victor's face darkened.

Zahira glanced from her husband to her father-in-law and back again, but Victor said nothing more. "I'll bring Cassandra and the baby as well," she assented in a timorous voice before walking hurriedly out of the room.

"And I will go tell Deborah to ready a tray of food for you," Victor volunteered. "You must have something to eat if you want to regain your strength."

Not long after his older son had left the room, one of Nathaniel's hands began clawing around, feeling his body and his bed for something he wasn't finding. "The locket," he wheezed. "Where is the locket?"

I leapt at the chance to make myself useful. If I didn't have the ability to make the man well again, at least I could help him be at peace. "The drawing room. It fell to the floor. Do you want me go get it?"

"Please," Nathaniel said in answer. He reached for Jameson's hand and clung to it. "Stay with me, my son," he implored.

"Of course," Jameson murmured, crouching down to draw level with his father.

I rushed out of the room and through the halls, tearing down the staircase and into the great hall. Despite the manner in which I had come to be involved with Nathaniel and his health, I couldn't help but feel guilty that I hadn't been able to help him more. Concern for the head of the Dorn family was weighing heavily on me, but I admit that in the back of my mind another thought was troubling me. Not only did I worry for Nathaniel, but I also worried about what would happen to me if he died. Nathaniel's passing would put Victor in charge as the new head of the family, and it was no secret how he felt about me.

Those were the thoughts pulsating through me, setting my limbs to quivering, as I jogged to the drawing room. Maybe it was the fact that I was so preoccupied when I entered the room that explains why the sight that greeted my eyes didn't sink in right away. I saw, but I didn't comprehend. Then all at once the numbness melted away and I realized I was looking at a corpse.

Sprawled on the floor of the drawing room was the inert form of the gardener, Tom. He lay on his side, strands of lank hair falling into his face. His lips were blue, the black tip of his tongue protruded from his mouth. His eyes bulged wide open. The bottoms of his work boots were caked with dirt and I thought inanely how furious Deborah and Frederick would be if they knew he had traipsed through the house with them.

"Oh, my god," I whispered.

My eyes found the glass tumbler. It had come to rest on the floor just beyond the gardener's hand, as though he had been holding it when he collapsed. Only trace amounts of amber liquid remained within. I quickly took stock of the other glasses, arranged around the room's tables where we had each set them. And I saw that it was Nathaniel's glass that the dead man had drunk from.

It finally clicked.

12

August 6th, 2013

When I began telling my tale I said that endings are often the start of something new. Such an optimistic view. I find it harder and harder to believe that these days. Something has ended and I can't see that I might ever start up again.

What is wrong with me? I can't even stand myself these days, with all the moping that I do.

I'm sure I'd feel better if I just got up and out, did something with myself. But I'm too tired right now. Maybe tomorrow.

When I rushed into Nathaniel's chambers I was flooded with relief to see that Victor had not yet returned. Jameson hadn't moved from his place kneeling at his father's bedside while I was gone from the room. Cassandra was now there, too, Wesley cradled in her arms. Zahira had left again to summon her own children.

"There you are, darling," Nathaniel said to his daughter. "You just missed your mother. She popped in for a visit."

Cassandra's eyebrows drew together. She looked to her brother for an explanation. Jameson lifted his eyes to mine and said in a quiet voice, "He began hallucinating shortly after you left the room."

I swallowed, my throat felt like sandpaper. "I think I know what's going on here," I blurted to the room at large. Brother and sister directed penetrating gazes my way. Nathaniel seemed to be in another world entirely. "I think your father is being poisoned." I told them about what I had discovered in the drawing room. In the midst of my explanation some composed corner of my mind realized that I had never actually retrieved the locket I had been sent for. "You said you can be killed by physical trauma, right? That murder among the Sentient wasn't unheard of? Whatever was in your father's glass tonight killed that man instantly. But he was only human. Your father's body is just putting up more of a fight."

They just stared. I think they were too stunned to know what to believe. I felt like it was crucial that I convince them. "Look, in that secret lab of yours. Are there any poisonous plant species?" If either of them wondered how I knew about the hidden room, they understood it was no time to question it.

It was Cassandra who answered. "Yes, a few. There's belladonna, foxglove, oleander..." Her voice trailed off. Her eyes were large and round as she began to bounce the baby distractedly in her arms. Wesley was sound asleep and I think the nervous gesture was more for her own sake.

"Victor has been pouring the drinks," Jameson said, his voice grim.

"I know he's...*Victor*, but do you really think he would go this far?" Cassandra posed, uncertain.

I had to tell them the other thought that had crossed my mind. "I think maybe he killed your mother too." Two sets of eyes snapped back in my direction. "Cassandra, you said Evelyn was with you when you overheard your mother talking about overruling the decree that passes power on to the oldest child in a family, right?

175

What if she told Victor what she had heard? How do you think he would have reacted to that news?"

"Your mother. Where is she?" Nathaniel's voice drifted over from where he lay. No one answered him, not knowing how.

Cassandra was looking at her brother. "Do you think...? Could it be?"

Jameson's whole body had stiffened. He was looking intently at the floor, as if racking his brain to determine if the horrific accusation could actually be true. "I think..." he began slowly. Then he looked up and said with resolve, "It makes sense. I think maybe Victor did kill her. And now he's trying to kill Father."

Nathaniel had overheard our conversation. "Victor killed Vivienne?" he repeated, drawing everyone's attention. He had pushed himself up onto his elbows and the look in his eyes was clearer than it had been just moments before.

"Father," Cassandra said, stepping closer to his bed.

Nathaniel looked at his daughter, and this time he truly saw her and the reality of the situation. He extended a pale arm and Cassandra slipped her hand into his. "Darling Cassandra," Nathaniel whispered. "I can never tell you how very sorry I am." His bleary eyes lit up as they greedily took in the sight of the sleeping infant in his daughter's arms.

Tears sprung to Cassandra's eyes. "I know," she whispered in turn.

Keeping his grasp on his daughter's hand, Nathaniel turned back to face Jameson and I. "Did you say Victor killed Vivienne?"

We were all reluctant to risk upsetting the man in his deteriorated state. However, the gaze he leveled at us seemed lucid enough now and there was no way we could just ignore such a question. I recounted my theory.

Nathaniel took time to take in everything I had said. A feverish hint of color had risen in his cheeks.

"Father," Cassandra murmured, drawing his attention to the fact that his grip on her hand had become uncomfortably tight. He apologized and released her hand. The old man had more strength left in him than we had given him credit for.

"This," he finally pronounced, "troubles me." Moments later he was struggling to drag his legs over the edge of the bed.

"Father, what are you doing?" Jameson asked.

"I must know if this is true," Nathaniel huffed as his feet dropped to the floor. My eyes locked with Jameson's, but neither of us could refuse him. Death drew nearer to the man every day, and before it took him he wanted to know if it was true, if his own son could be responsible for these crimes. I knew how important this man's dignity was to him, whatever shreds of it were left hanging from his weakened frame. He would want to be standing for this confrontation, to meet his opponent head on. I stepped to his side and gave him my arm for support. "Where is Victor?"

"He went to get you something to eat," I answered.

"Or is it something more to poison him with?" Jameson wondered aloud. He and Cassandra followed along behind me and Nathaniel as we tottered toward the door.

It was slow going, and with each labored step we took it felt as though my heart beat faster and faster. I jerked back involuntarily when we were surprised by Zahira, Evelyn and Julian rounding a corner in the halls and nearly running into us. Zahira startled as well.

"What's going on?" she asked. No one bothered to answer. She and the children fell into step behind us.

When we reached the stairs, there at the foot was Victor, just starting to skip up the steps when he spotted us. He carried a tray in his hands. On it was a soup tureen with steam escaping around the edges of the lid. Next to the covered dish was a portion of bread, with a knife for slicing it and a slab of butter.

"What is this?" Victor demanded to know, continuing up the steps.

Nathaniel had seized the banister at the top of the stairs. I knew he would want me to let go of his arm, to allow him as much face as possible for this encounter, but I wouldn't. Not when he was so unsteady. The others had come to form a half-circle behind us, watching. Wary.

"Father, you mustn't be out of bed so soon. There's no telling when you'll have another fit like that last one. Here, I've brought food to fortify yourself with. Consider it your dinner, seeing as you never even touched yours tonight."

"Is it dinner, or is it more poison to finish him off with?" Jameson asked scathingly.

Victor had almost reached the top of the staircase. He narrowed his eyes at his brother. "What are you going on about now?"

It was Nathaniel who responded. Without preamble he asked his son, "Did you kill your mother?"

Victor had reached the top step and stood just below his father. His eyes widened. "*What* did you say?"

"Did you kill your mother?"

Victor was struck speechless. He looked to his wife but her eyes were fixed on her father-in-law, aghast. Victor's brow scrunched over his eyes as he replied to the allegation.

"You truly believe I would have killed my own mother?" He glanced toward Jameson. "What, and that now I am poisoning my father?" He barked out a harsh laugh. "You all think me capable of such a thing?"

Again, Nathaniel, his even tone never changing, only said, "Did you kill your mother?" Victor's glower deepened. Those of us watching didn't dare breathe.

"Father."

"Did you kill her?"

"Father!"

"*Did you kill my wife?*"

Victor hissed. "What do you think?"

At first all I was aware of was Nathaniel lunging forward and almost toppling down the stairs. He dragged me forward with him, and my heart leapt to my throat before I caught my balance and stumbled back a few steps, pulling Nathaniel with me. Only then did my brain process what I had just witnessed. Nathaniel had snatched up the knife from the food tray and driven it into Victor's chest.

Victor didn't seem to understand what had happened right away either. His eyes grew wide, and looked down to his chest. He watched as the crimson stole across the front of his shirt from the point where the knife handle protruded. Nathaniel tugged the blade out and it was then Victor crumpled. The tray crashed to the floor and spun away down the stairs, leaving a trail of food in its wake. Victor slid down the staircase, his head jarring as it struck each step along the way.

It was when Victor first dropped that the others began to realize what had happened. I heard a gasp behind me, and someone cried out. But it was the ear-piercing shrieking that froze my blood. It sounded like it was being ripped up and out of someone's chest and through a mouth that barely paused for a breath. Horrified, I spun around and saw that it was coming from Evelyn. She had her hands dug into her scalp and was pulling her hair straight out above her head. Still screeching, she flew down the stairs to where her father's body had come to rest at the bottom. She flung her body over his. After releasing a few shuddering sobs she swung her head around to look up at us, her red and tear-stained face transformed with rage.

"It was *me*, you fools!" she wailed. "*I* killed her! I pushed her down the damn stairs, and now I've been trying to get rid of him!" She jutted her quivering chin toward her grandfather. "Pathetic fools, all of you!" She leaned over Victor. His eyes had seemed to bulge as she spoke. I don't know if it was in response to his daughter's admission, or maybe that's just when the last of his life was torn from his body. From then on his sightless eyes never left the ceiling high above. All color drained from his face, from everywhere, as the pool of blood around him grew.

It was then I noticed Nathaniel was trembling. I gave a gentle tug on his arm and steered him over to the wall where he could prop himself up for support. The shaking only grew more violent, and the bloodied knife slipped out of his grasp and dropped to the floor. He clapped his hands to the sides of his head.

The baby had begun to squall amidst all of the commotion. Looking to the others I saw that Julian's mouth was stretched open, his eyes crinkled and droplets formed at the tip of his nose ready to plummet at any moment. His grief made no sound. His mother stood transfixed, staring with horror toward the bottom of the stairs. Seeing she was in no condition to help her son, Cassandra intervened. She placed an arm around the boy's shoulders and led him away down the hall. The sound of Wesley's crying faded as they went.

I came to stand next to Jameson at the top of the stairs. Evelyn had resumed her keening and we watched as she rocked back and forth over her father's corpse. In the meantime, both Deborah and Frederick appeared, likely having been drawn by all the noise. The housekeeper let out a cry and spun away, turning her back to the grisly scene. Frederick gaped in disbelief.

"What happens now?" I asked Jameson under my breath.

He gritted his teeth so fiercely that I could hear the grinding. The looks that crossed his face were unreadable, and I knew he must be experiencing many different feelings all at once. "First things first," he answered after a minute. He stomped down the steps, footfalls heavy with purpose. He wrapped his arms tightly around Evelyn's own, pinning them to her sides, and hauled her up from her vigil. Her screaming rekindled, surging to even greater volumes, and she kicked her feet wildly as her uncle lugged her away from her father's body. Her weight seemed like nothing in Jameson's arms, although he did take several vicious blows from her heels against his shins. He carried her up the stairs and away down the corridor. Zahira watched them go, rooted to the spot. I guessed that the girl was to be confined, much like Cassandra had been, until her fate was decided. What was the penalty for murder among the Sentient?

I threw one last look down the stairs to where Victor's body lay in a heap. The man had been a bastard, but apparently not as much of a bastard as we had suspected. And now he was dead for crimes he did not actually commit. At his own father's hand no less.

A pang of guilt stabbed through me for coming to the wrong conclusion about Victor, as had everyone else. I felt worse for Nathaniel, though. The poor man was all but broken already, and now he had to face what he had done. I had never expected such violence from him, and had to wonder how much of his failing health and deteriorating mental state had come into play in his decision to act as he had.

At that moment I heard a soft moan come from behind me. I had managed to forget that Nathaniel himself was still there, huddled against the wall with his hands now covering his face.

I crossed over to him.

"What have I done? What have we all done?" he lamented in a frail voice. "None of this, none of it should ever have come to be. My family. Where did it all go so wrong?"

I had no answers for him. I met no resistance as I helped him to his feet and accompanied him back to his room. Once I had the old man settled on the sofa in his sitting room, he looked to the portrait of his wife and the tears began spilling down his face. Even in the short time I had known the man, his illness had drawn crags along his face, a reflection of how withered he had become on the inside. I was aware that no kind words or assurances I could offer him would penetrate his grief right then, but I had to do something. I lowered myself onto the sofa next to Nathaniel and held his hand in mine while he wept. After a time he dried his cheeks with the sleeve of his shirt, reminding me at that moment of nothing so much as an overgrown boy. An overgrown, preternatural, frightened little boy with his spirit shattered.

He angled his head in my direction. "I want to thank you, Miss Cassidy. For everything."

I didn't feel like I had done much. In fact, I was partly responsible for the ugly turn of events with Victor. However, I didn't have the energy or the will to argue. I felt hollow on the inside and numb around the edges. There were two dead bodies in the house, and two murderers. That seemed like quite enough to deal with in one night and I hesitated to allow anything else in.

I drew my hands from Nathaniel's and gave his shoulder a squeeze. I stood and walked out, and retreated to my own room. For what little it was worth, I locked myself inside.

More than an hour must have passed. I didn't do much that entire time but sit cross-legged on the bed, petting Dinah absentmindedly, while caught up in the whirlwind raging through my mind. I think I was trying to sort through everything that had been happening, to understand how my life had to come to that point. I don't know that I had made much progress in figuring it out before I heard the knocking at my door.

When I stood to answer the door I realized how bone-tired I was. With a sigh, I unlocked the door and pulled it open.

Jameson stood in the doorway, arms braced on the either side of the threshold. His shadowed face looked as weary as I felt. "Are you alright?" he asked. His voice sounded hoarse, worn out.

I stepped back and motioned for him to enter.

"What's going to happen?" I asked over my shoulder. Jameson settled himself in the chair at my desk before answering.

"With Evelyn? I don't know for sure." He shook his head. "Cassandra was always the most talented with the spagyrics. She thinks...hopes that now that Father will receive no more poison, his body may be able to start to repair itself. As long as it's not too late, she believes he might make a full recovery."

That might be true, physically. But how does one recover from misguidedly killing one's own child? And discovering that your granddaughter murdered your wife? The Dorn family was harboring more dark secrets than it had ever anticipated.

"And you needn't worry about Cassandra," Jameson went on. "She has her freedom back. Under the circumstances, even if our father had the will to keep her detained any longer I don't think he would consider himself in the position to demand it. I don't think he wants that anymore, anyway."

We fell quiet. After a time I asked, "How will you explain your brother's death to the others?"

"I don't know yet. But at least now we have a reasonable explanation for Father's sickness to give before the deadline they assigned. Not that divulging the truth will be our family's proudest moment." Now it was Jameson's turn to heave a sigh. "Regardless, you don't need to concern yourself any longer." He stood as if it required more effort than usual, then took the few steps to bring him to where I sat on the edge of the bed. He ran a hand lightly down the length my hair, rubbing the ends between his fingers. "We want to thank you for all you have done to help us here. But from here on you may consider the Dorn family no longer your problem." Did that mean that, with Victor gone, I no longer had to fear for my own safety? I couldn't imagine Nathaniel and his two remaining children being willing to harm me in any way. They had each shown me kindness during my time at their home, albeit in curious ways fitting the unusual circumstances of my stay. I was hopeful, I was distraught. There were too many emotions to hang onto any one of them. Instead, I closed my eyes and leaned into his hand, narrowing my awareness down to the feel of Jameson's fingers through my hair. The other feelings could wait.

After a couple of minutes he pulled away, and when I opened my eyes he was gone.

That night I slept like the dead. I woke sometime in the late morning to a profound silence. The cat lay spread out at the foot of my bed, still asleep. Recollection of the previous evening's events flooded over me all at once and I curled up into a ball. There were many ways I had envisioned my time at Willow Glen drawing to an end, most of them less than pleasant. This, however, was not one I had been able to imagine and I was at a complete loss as to how to feel. I realize now that I was still in a state of shock, and wasn't yet able to feel much of anything at all. What I wanted most of all was to stay in the illusory safety of my blankets. I couldn't ignore the hunger pains that were shooting through my belly for long, though. It was with regret that I tore myself from bed and got dressed.

I held my breath as I approached the staircase but saw to my relief that no evidence of Victor's death remained. No splattered soup, no blood, no body. Still, I chose my steps carefully as I descended into the great hall.

There was no spread of food left out as there usually was for breakfast, but I wasn't surprised. Like the rest of us, Deborah had experienced quite a shock the night before. Maybe they had actually taken pity on the housekeeper and lightened her duties, or relieved her of them altogether for the day. I hoped the real explanation wasn't something far more sinister.

I found the kitchen empty as well. I rifled through the cupboards and drawers and helped myself to a croissant, hoping Deborah wouldn't mind. Out of some morbid sense of curiosity I headed for the drawing room while I bit into the flaky bread.

As I suspected, the body of the gardener had been removed as well. The glasses had been cleaned away, everything was in its rightful place. The locket was nowhere in sight.

I thought suddenly of Nathaniel and self-reproach washed over me. He was my patient, of sorts, after all. I might not have been able to handle any more the night before, but there was no reason I couldn't check in on the man in the morning. Stuffing the last of the croissant into my mouth, I left the drawing room and headed for Nathaniel's chambers.

I tapped my knuckles on the door, pushed it open and peered inside. I was taken aback to see the rooms were empty, the bed neatly made. I wondered if the Sentient body was capable of healing itself even faster than I had imagined. I navigated through the sitting room over to the glass door to the balcony and slid it open. Nathaniel was not there either. The garden spread out beneath me looking as enchanting as ever, as did the vista beyond it. But there was nobody there.

That was when the tingling sensation began to creep up my spine.

My pace quickened as I searched through the hallways, in Cassandra's room, down to the parlor, the library. All empty. I walked to the hidden door amid the bookshelves but it was firmly shut and gave no hint of the secrets behind it. I brushed my hand over the alchemical symbol on the wall, feeling my heart sink.

After some more furious searching I finally accepted what had become increasingly evident.

I had been left all alone in Willow Glen Manor.

13

August 7th, 2013

I'm sorry to say that's the end of my story. Not much of an ending, is it? I know. Believe me, I know.

Throughout the rest of that day and those that followed, I waited half-expectantly for one of the Dorns or their servants to return and explain their absence. That never happened. And here I still am, just me and my cat by ourselves in Willow Glen, roaming its halls like lost lambs. Okay, maybe not so much Dinah, she rather likes having the run of the house these days. But I find myself searching high and low for some sign, some clue of where they might have gone. Sometimes when I stand out on the terrace gazing into the shifting branches and leaves of the overgrown garden, I think I see someone moving out of the corner of my eye. I have come to realize that in my desolation my mind is playing tricks on me, showing me what I wish to see.

One thing I did find was an envelope full of cash left on the side table in the great hall. A lot of cash. With it was a note addressed to me that said it was "for services rendered in the matter of Nathaniel Dorn's health." Well, I'm glad it clarified at least which services were being referred to.

With all the time I've had on my hands I've been able to go over it all in my mind again and again, everything that's happened to me since my chance encounter with Cassandra Dorn, which now seems like it took place an eternity ago. I see now how in the drawing room after dinner Evelyn always insisted on serving Nathaniel his brandy, acting as if she was doting on her ailing grandfather. In reality she must have been slipping something nefarious into his drinks. And of course, she was the one who drew up the mixture that was supposed to have the same therapeutic effects as the medication people took for heart failure. Who knows what was actually in that vial? I'm betting she was the one who left me that bracelet, too, although I still wouldn't put that past her father. Even if he wasn't conspiring patricide, he certainly made it clear that he wanted me out of the picture.

Cassandra had named some of the poisonous plants that are kept in Willow Glen's conservatory. Belladonna, foxglove, and oleander, she had said. I browsed through the library during one of these solitary days of mine and located a book on botany. When I read that the genus name for foxglove was *digitalis,* bells alarmed in my head. From working on adult floors in the hospital as a nursing student, I knew that many patients in heart failure take a drug called Digoxin. I also remembered the term for when too much of it collected in a person's bloodstream: digitalis toxicity. The symptoms are an awful lot like those that Nathaniel was experiencing. Not only the effects on his body but also the depression, the disorientation and hallucinating at the very end. I'm willing to bet that foxglove was at least part of what his granddaughter had been doling out to him.

In retrospect I see that Evelyn shared all the same reasons we suspected Victor held to want to kill Nathaniel and Vivienne. As the eldest child of the eldest child, she stood to lose just as much as he did if the standards of ascendency were revised. And certainly she seemed to hang on her father's every word, so it follows that she also had little regard for her grandfather's way of presiding over the family. I didn't envy the family having to sort through all of that mess.

With all this time to stumble around astray in my own thoughts, I even think I understand why they all left like they did. Nathaniel had once told me that the Dorns owned several estates around the world, and in the family's time of crisis they may have fled to one of those other places. It had been alluded to that humans who knew too much about the Sentient were either kept on in their service for life, or else eliminated. I, on the other hand, had been allowed a chance to reclaim my own life. I think Nathaniel may have granted me my life in exchange for having helped to save his. I suppose I should feel grateful. Instead, I just feel abandoned.

It's like I had been offered a glimpse into another world, maybe not a fairytale world, but certainly a captivating one. And then it had been ripped away.

I realize I am being kind of silly here. I mean, I have no place in that world. And after the things I've witnessed, why should I want to? If anything, I should be elated that things turned out as well as they did for me, considering the alternatives that had been looming over my head for weeks. No way should I be hurt, comparing myself to a dog's used up chew toy, tossed to the side and forgotten. Expendable once again.

Anyway. Enough moping. I thought that writing this account down would help me sort through it all and understand why I have been feeling the way I have, how I *should* be feeling about it all. But I'm just as lost as ever. Regardless, I know that I can't stay hidden away here in this mansion all by myself forever. I have to return to the land of the living sometime. Resume my own, real life. Soon.

But I'm just not ready yet.

I'm sorry if my story has been a disappointment to you. All I can say is, try living it. That's it. This is the end.

14

August 10th, 2013

The last time I made an entry in this journal I wrote that my story had come to an end. It turns out that's not true. In fact, I think this is just the beginning.

Maybe you guessed it before I did; it wouldn't be the first time that has happened. I can only argue that I had other things on my mind.

Yesterday I was idling listlessly in bed like usual, without the energy to do much else and not feeling well besides. And then something occurred to me. My period was late.

I knew it could have just been that my body hadn't regulated itself totally yet after the miscarriage. But then again there was the fatigue, the tears at the drop of a hat...

There was a jumble of emotions swarming around inside of me as I steeled myself for another foray into the real world. I drove into town just long enough to scoop up an armful of pregnancy tests, then returned here with them.

I was too anxious to wait for the next morning to test, like the boxes said to. Besides, I had bought six of the damn things. So I ripped into the foil packaging of the first stick and tested right away. In no time at all the color swept across the little window, and there was the plus sign: immediate, bold, and undeniable.

I tried another one. It said yes, too.

Let's just say throughout the rest of the day and this morning too I have been making a lot of trips to the bathroom. And every time it has been confirmed.

I am having a baby.

Of course I have a lot of mixed feelings about this. There's a hint of fear that I might miscarry, although I had been assured that there is no reason to assume it would happen again. There's a twinge of sadness for the other baby, the one who never had a chance. There's the trepidation that accompanies an unplanned pregnancy and the knowledge that now I have to make a life suitable to bring up a baby in. And of course there's the fact that I haven't know the father for very long and have absolutely no idea where in the world he might be right now.

But mostly there is pure, unrestrained joy.

I am having a baby.

I don't know where exactly I will go from here, but I do know that, finally, I am ready. Ready to move on, to take the reins and pick up my own life again. To make a new life.

Because I am having a baby.

A baby with Sentient blood in its veins.

ABOUT THE AUTHOR

Jessica Crawford lives in Upstate New York with her husband, their two awesome little boys, two cats, a goldfish, and a snail. She works as a registered nurse in a NICU. Writing has been a lifelong passion of hers. You can visit her blog at http://jessicacrawfordwrites.blogspot.com/

Made in the USA
Charleston, SC
18 May 2014